❧ All for One ❧

Don't miss the other books in the Definitely Dominguita series!

#1: *Knight of the Cape*
#2: *Captain Dom's Treasure*

Coming soon:
#4: *Sherlock Dom*

Definitely
DOMINGUITA
❧ All for One ❧

By
Terry Catasús Jennings
Illustrated by
Fátima Anaya

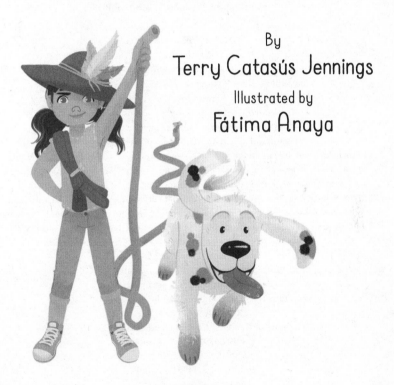

ALADDIN
New York London Toronto Sydney New Delhi

ALADDIN

An imprint of Simon & Schuster Children's Publishing Division
1230 Avenue of the Americas, New York, New York 10020
First Aladdin hardcover edition August 2021
Text copyright © 2021 by Terry Catasús Jennings
Illustrations copyright © 2021 by Fátima Anaya
Also available in an Aladdin paperback edition.
All rights reserved, including the right of reproduction in whole or in part in any form.
ALADDIN and related logo are registered trademarks of Simon & Schuster, Inc.
For information about special discounts for bulk purchases, please contact
Simon & Schuster Special Sales at 1-866-506-1949 or business@simonandschuster.com.
The Simon & Schuster Speakers Bureau can bring authors to your live event. For more
information or to book an event contact the Simon & Schuster Speakers Bureau
at 1-866-248-3049 or visit our website at www.simonspeakers.com.
Book designed by Heather Palisi
The illustrations for this book were rendered digitally.
The text of this book was set in Candida.
Manufactured in the United States of America 0721 FFG
2 4 6 8 10 9 7 5 3 1
Library of Congress Control Number 2021930778
ISBN 9781534465121(hc)
ISBN 9781534465114 (pbk)
ISBN 9781534465138 (ebook)

To every one of us who loves to pretend

—T. C. J.

To Memito and Sofi

—F. A.

Contents

The Library Book

Dominguita Melendez stepped into the library wearing her grandmother's pamela—her favorite. She doffed the wide-brimmed floppy hat when she reached the librarian.

"Musketeer?" Mrs. Booker peered over her reading glasses to look at Dom. "Is that your next adventure?"

Dom decided to use musketeer words. "Forsooth! How'd you guess?" she said. "My hat doesn't even have a feather!"

"Forsooth, indeed. You reserved *The Three Musketeers* last night—dead giveaway." The librarian stood up to get the book. "Besides, not too many people come into the library wearing a wide-brimmed velvet hat with or without feathers."

"Good point. We'll study the book carefully tonight. We'll be ready for an adventure this weekend."

"You're missing the rest of your crew."

"Pancho had a dentist appointment after school. Steph is at the leg doctor—she's getting a smaller brace. I'm meeting them later. And we already know a lot about the musketeers. About recovering the queen's diamonds, the decoys at the fort, and all the duels. But we want to refresh our memories. Need to make sure we get our musketeer talk down pat."

"So you're going with three?"

Dom knew that *The Three Musketeers* was not just about *three* musketeers. They had a friend. She shrugged. "It doesn't really matter, right?"

"Not at all," the librarian agreed.

"Jim Hawkins was the main character in *Treasure Island*, and none of us decided to be him."

"And you could always change your mind later."

"Yeah. My brother Rafi's always wanting to join in. He loves *The Three Musketeers* too." Dom leaned in close to the librarian. "He's still writing about us for our abuela, you know."

Mrs. Booker smiled. "Can't wait to read the newest adventure."

Dom put her hat back on. "I'm on the way to Fuentes Salvage to get our equipment. We're meeting tonight to make our plans. I'll bring the book back soon."

"No rush. You have three weeks."

With that, Dom was off.

2
The Equipment Quest

At Fuentes Salvage, pots, pans, spatulas, dish towels, trash cans—anything for the house, especially for the kitchen—were scattered around in huge piles.

In the messy front room.

In the dusty back room.

All the way to the loading dock.

"Dominguita! How sweet! Rafi sent you to help us!" It was Leni, el Señor Fuentes's granddaughter. Her eyes sparkled. Some black curls had escaped over her forehead from the pile perched on top of her head.

Leni was wrong. Rafi hadn't asked Dom to come. He'd left for school before she had, and she hadn't seen him all day. The only reason she was at the junk store was to borrow stuff for the musketeer adventure.

But musketeers were helpful, and el Señor Fuentes had let Dom borrow all sorts of equipment before. And Rafi was about to escort Leni that weekend at her quinceañera party—to celebrate her fifteenth birthday. Dom would definitely help. "I'm most happy to be of assistance, kind lady."

Leni raised her hands, palms up. "That's great, because he bought a storage unit!"

"A storage unit?"

"A soggy one," she said, holding up a drippy dish towel. "It belonged to a kitchen supply store. Water got into the unit, and a lot of the stuff in it was damaged." Leni swept her arms over the mess. "He bought it all, and here we are! He's been working on it all day!"

"And I'll make a lot of money, Dom." El Señor Fuentes dumped a trash can full of stuff onto the floor. He got down to Dom's level. His arm pointed. The eyebrow over his blue eye danced. "You see those vacuum cleaners over there by the wall? They're worth two hundred dollars new. And they weren't damaged in the flood. If I get as little as twenty-five dollars for each, I'll make a hundred bucks. If I sell those four, which I know I will, everything else is gravy."

"Oh." Dom nodded. She could do the math. But she would probably charge more than twenty-five dollars for the vacuum cleaners. Her mom had just paid more than a hundred for her new one.

"The big deal is that a lot of the boxes got wet and damp. Some things got dirty. But there's nothing wrong with them."

"And you can sell them?"

"A regular store, the one that this belonged to, can't sell damaged goods." The eyebrow over the brown eye rose, to make the point. "But people expect the stuff I sell to be old and damaged! I charge less for it. I can even put it on the internet!"

Leni swiped the air. "FuentesSalvage.com!"

"Claro que sí, señorita. And I'll make enough so I can pay for that fancy party you're having this weekend!"

Leni twirled, then gave her granddad a big hug. "Yes! I can't wait for the music and dancing! And flowers and cake! You're the best!"

Dom was happy to help, for el Señor Fuentes and because she was a musketeer. But she couldn't spend forever. She was meeting the rest of the musketeers at five. It was almost three.

First, she set aside Abuela's pamela carefully on a cleanish shelf. Then she took over for Leni outside, helping el Señor Fuentes wring and dry things. Leni grouped and organized things inside.

By four, everything was out of the truck and in neat piles. Some of it was stashed on shelves.

"We deserve a treat!" Leni said. She reached into a small refrigerator for a can and poured a stream of thick, creamy condensed milk into three plastic cups. She added a can of ice-cold Malta Hatuey soda to each cup, stirred them all, and tasted one. "Yum." She handed them around.

El Señor Fuentes took a big gulp. "Ah!" he said, sitting on the floor, leaning against the checkout counter. "It doesn't get any better than this."

Dom licked her lips. Malta Hatuey with condensed milk was like an ice-cream float—without the ice cream. So sweet it made your teeth tingle. "I'm in heaven," she declared.

"And what are you today, Dom?" El Señor Fuentes wiped a condensed-milk mustache off his upper lip.

"Musketeer," Dom said, licking hers.

El Señor Fuentes swept the store with his hand. "Take your pick."

Dom found something called a cobweb duster— she could tell from the cardboard it was attached to. It was a perfect plume for a musketeer hat. Except half of it dangled in her hand when she picked it up. It didn't bother Dom a bit. Each half might be a tad short for a musketeer hat, but it was good enough—one for Steph and one for Pancho. They'd love the fuzzy stumps. "These will be good for making baldrics," she told Leni.

"Baldrics?"

"Something to stick your weapons in. Kind of like a sash, or a belt."

"Hmmm." Leni knotted two dish towels together at a corner, twirled the whole thing into a rope, and wrapped it around her waist. She even left a tail hanging from one side. She posed. "What do you think?"

"Perfect. But I want mine over my shoulder."

"Ooh! I have something you'll love." Leni leaned down behind a glass case and pulled out a beautiful golden tie clip studded with clear stones. She folded two purple dish towels and joined them together. She draped them over Dom's shoulder.

Dom posed.

"Perfect! And I have two more. You can all rock your baldrics!"

Dom could see why Rafi liked Leni so much. She wouldn't mind having Leni be a musketeer, if Leni wanted to.

The only other thing left to find were swords for dueling. Dom looked around again.

And she found them.

Next to toilet paper holders and bathroom trash cans.

Plungers!

Plungers could work like musketeer swords

when you turned them—handle side forward—and slid the plunger in—so you could hold the handle. The plungers could work well enough even though they were fat, not skinny. And short, not long. She was set.

"These aren't damaged at all," Dom said.

"Take them!" Leni said.

"Thank you! Thank you! Thank you!" Dom exclaimed. "I'll bring everything back when we're done being musketeers."

"No, thank *you*! Before you came we had a pile of junk. Now we have *highly organized* junk!" Leni bowed. "You made it easier for us."

Dom carefully stashed the plungers in the bottom of a reusable grocery bag she found—she wanted to surprise her crew. She stuffed the rest of her loot on top and snapped the two tie clips to an open pocket inside the bag—carefully.

"Is there any other way I can be of service?" she asked with a bow before she left.

"As a matter of fact, kind Musketeer," el Señor Fuentes said. "If you could take a check to Tava's

Butcher for us, that would allow us to finish here."

Dom nodded. "Of course. It's on my way."

El Señor Fuentes looked at his watch. "I promised Antonio Tava that I would have the check to him by four thirty." Then he leaned his head close to Dom's and whispered, "I want everything to be perfect for Leni's quinceañera, you know. Her grandmother never had one. I didn't have enough money when Leni's mother turned fifteen, either. Everything must be perfect. You only turn fifteen once!"

"No need to worry," Dom said. She already knew the other big reason el Señor Fuentes wanted everything to be perfect—it was just the two of them now. Leni's parents died in a car accident when she was little, and her grandmother had died two years ago.

"You can count on me. Musketeer's honor," Dom declared. "I will help you make Leni's party the best ever. I will take the check. I will not allow the party pigs to be in peril. You can trust me."

A Familiar Dastardliness

"Do you know a chicken landed on your head?" The teenager behind the butcher shop counter wore a bloody apron. The name tag on the strap said VINNIE.

Dom patted her pamela, now grandly decorated with feathers from the soggy storage unit. "I'm a musketeer."

Vinnie took in the costume, and his face curled into a snarl. Like a hyena's. "Ooh, ooh! A musketeer."

She tried to ignore the snarl. "I'm here to pay for pigs."

"Well, then, featherhead," Vinnie said. "Pay for the pigs."

She had heard those words before. Or something really close. And she knew in her gut it hadn't ended well that other time. She couldn't stop to think about it, though. This was an urgent mission. She had to give the payment to Mr. Tava, the owner, by 4:30. It was exactly 4:17. She showed the snarling boy the check.

"I need to see Mr. Tava. El Señor Fuentes said I should."

"The junkyard man?"

The hair on the back of Dom's neck stood at attention. What was it with the guy? On top of being the supplier of all her equipment, el Señor Fuentes was her abuela's good friend. And Rafi and Leni were best friends. "My man, you know not of what you speak. I need to see Mr. Tava. *Now.*"

"He's not here," Vinnie sang, his head bobbing in time to the words.

"No way! I need to make the payment."

"So make it. I can take the check."

"You're not Mr. Tava. El Señor Fuentes told me to give it to Mr. Tava."

"And Mr. Tava told me to take the check, featherhead."

Something felt terribly wrong. The boy's laugh. The hyena snarl. Did she know them? They made her toes curl. But she didn't take time to figure it out. Even though every bone in her body went against it, she didn't have any choice. El Señor Fuentes had promised to have the check at the butcher's by four thirty. If she didn't pay for the pigs, she would let him down. She put the check on the counter.

Vinnie took it.

"I need a receipt or something," Dom said. "Something to prove I gave you the check. And what time I gave it to you."

"As you wish." The boy pulled out a dirty sheet of paper and started writing. As he wrote, he left a gross streak of blood on the paper. "What's your name?"

Ugh! She hated the blood, but she couldn't worry about that. "Write this down. The money's from Emilio Fuentes."

"You want an official receipt? I need your name." Vinnie started to crumple the paper.

"No, no, no. Wait," Dom blurted out. "It's Dominguita. Dominguita Melendez."

The snarl got even nastier. "Melendez, huh? You Rafi Melendez's sister?"

Wait, how did he know Rafi?

The snarling boy took her mind away from the

16

question. "So this is for Little Sunday Melendez?" he asked.

Grrr! Why had her parents named her after a day of the week? It created all sorts of problems. "You can call me Dom."

"Why would I want to call you anything?"

All Dom wanted to do right that second was straighten up that snarl. And put a cork in that mouth.

But the boy with the hyena snarl was twice as tall as she was.

And as old as her brother.

And her dueling sword was out of reach, in the bag.

"Can you just write the receipt?" She needed proof she'd paid for the pigs by four thirty, and she needed it now. She wasn't about to make him angry.

Vinnie leaned on the counter. "So how's Leni doing? The queen of Mundytown High School?"

Huh? Why was he talking about Leni? Why didn't he just write the receipt? Dom wasn't about to tell him anything. Especially since his voice dripped with nastiness.

She tapped her finger on the piece of paper. "Please write down 'three suckling pigs for Emilio Fuentes.' And put there that we've paid."

"Chill, Little Sunday, chill." Snarly Face scribbled on the piece of paper. He finished with PAID in big letters across the page.

"That's not all. El Señor Prieto at Yuca, Yuca will be picking them up. All three of them. He's the one who's cooking them." She searched every corner of her brain. Was there anything she was forgetting? "And put down that I got here at four seventeen and gave you the check at"—she looked at her phone—"at four twenty-two p.m. today."

"Of course, Little Sunday. Your wish is my command." Vinnie bowed and put the check and the receipt in the drawer.

She had done everything she was supposed to do. Why did her gut tell her Vinnie, who looked so familiar, knew something she didn't, and that her life would depend on it?

The Musketeer Swords

"Hallooo there, trusty steed!" Dom opened the gate and let the dog into Steph's yard. Roco was the musketeers' roving pet. He had been their steed during their knightly adventures. He'd also helped Dom with Juan Largo during their treasure hunt. Most of the time Roco stayed at the Holland House Restaurant, where he had an endless supply of food scraps. But sometimes, when he was in the neighborhood, he stopped at Steph's house.

Finding Roco at Steph's house was perfect. Musketeers had steeds too, didn't they?

"I'm so happy to see you!" She reached down to give him a good scratch between the ears. As she nuzzled him, she heard the door open. And she smelled fresh-baked cookies.

"I think we need to go inside, dear steed," she said, and led Roco up onto the porch and through the door. Roco headed for the kitchen as if he lived there.

"Holy guacamole!" Pancho said. "I like that hat!" Pancho was tall, with hair that looked as if it hadn't seen a comb in weeks.

Dom posed. "Abuela's pamela—she wore it when she was a princess in the Mundytown Easter Parade."

"Abuela's pahwhat?" Steph said. Red bangs covered her forehead. All you could see of her face was a pair of bright-blue eyes and a tic-tac-toe of freckles dancing on her cheeks.

"Pah-MEH-lah. It's a floppy hat with a wide brim. It's like the girl's name except the accent's in the middle."

"Why don't you just say 'hat'?"

"Because with one word you cover four—wide-brimmed floppy hat. Besides," Dom said, "that's what Abuela called it, so that's what I'll call it."

"Love the feathers," Pancho said.

Dom pulled the cobweb dusters and the not-too-soggy and tattered feather dusters out of her bag. "Got some for you, too!"

The musketeers got to work on their costumes.

Steph picked half of the cobweb duster and two green feathers that were fairly straight. She attached them to one of her Gran's old gardening hats. Gray twine held them in place.

Pancho picked a usable feather from the green duster and plucked a second feather from a goldish one. He stuck the ends of the two feathers through the chin-strap hole on his grandfather's bowler hat and angled them just so. Stepping back to admire his work, he shook his head.

"That fuzzy thing," he told Steph. "That's awesome!" He added the other half of a teal cobweb duster, then smiled. White velvet ribbon completed the look.

After seeing how good Steph's and Pancho's

colorful feathers looked, Dom replaced two of her white feathers with brighter ones. One teal and the second one golden brown. She wrapped a nicely matching pink cord around the crown of her pamela.

"Now for the baldrics," Dom said, pulling out the dishcloths.

She modeled the one she'd made with Leni's help. She handed out the tie clips. "Can you believe Leni let me borrow these? I think the stones are diamonds. They look real, don't they?"

Pancho and Steph both nodded enthusiastically. Roco barked his approval.

Dom lifted out the two dish towels Leni had knotted together. "You could do it this way to go around your waist, or do a sash over your shoulder like I did."

Pancho and Steph also decided on sashes. Steph chose watermelon-colored towels that almost matched Gran's hat. Pancho chose olive green. Maybe they were more like hand towels instead of dishcloths. But they were unmistakably elegant.

"I think we need a picture," Steph said, eyeing herself in the mirror. "This is the fanciest costume ever."

Pancho disagreed. "Not yet. We need dueling swords," he said, looking at Dom. "What if somebody challenges us to a duel!"

With a flourish, Dom pulled a plunger from the bottom of the bag.

"Plungers?!" Steph and Pancho yelled at the same time.

"Not plungers. Épées. Musketeer swords. Perfect for dueling."

"Musketeer swords are long and skinny," Pancho pointed out.

Dom shrugged. "And these are short and fat. You got any better ones?"

"Who cares what they look like!" Steph scrunched her nose as if she'd smelled something awful. "They're gross and icky! UGH."

Dom reminded Steph about the flooding of the storage unit and el Señor Fuentes's good luck in getting a lot of brand-new (and wet) things for nothing.

Pancho cut his eyes at Dom. "You think anyone will be afraid of a clean plunger? It would have been better if they *really* were gross."

All three musketeers stopped. For a second.

Steph finally broke the silence. "What if . . . ," she said. "What if we turn them the right way and point the 'dirty' end at whoever we're attacking."

"Hmmm." Dom turned her plunger around.

"Hmmm," Pancho said. "Might work, but they need to be gross."

"We have Gran's cookies," Steph said. "The chocolate's still warm . . . and soft . . . and *brown*!"

Pancho looked longingly at the cookies before he

smeared the soft chocolate over his plunger. Steph and Dom bit a few pieces off before grossing up theirs.

In less than five minutes, all three of them had transformed their swords into the ickiest dueling swords ever. With bits of cookie crumbs embedded in the chocolate.

"En guarde," Dom said, one arm behind her and up, the other wielding her gross plunger.

"En poop," Pancho said, and he met her thrust with his plunger.

"En poop," they all said.

"One for all and all for one!"

They called Roco into the living room and asked Steph's gran to take a picture with Dom's phone—the phone Dom was allowed to use if she was abducted by aliens or if she needed to tell her mom that she'd gotten home.

Once the picture was done, they put their plungers on a cookie sheet to dry and sat down to make plans.

But they didn't get very far.

Dom's phone rang. It was her brother, and he was MAD.

"Why didn't you take the check to the butcher?" Rafi yelled.

"I dropped it off at Tava's Butcher at four twenty-two." Dom reached into her pocket to get the receipt, but she couldn't find it. She was so upset she forgot to use her musketeer words. "Oh no! The guy working there had me so twisted around, I left the receipt. No worries. I'll run by and get it and bring it to you."

"Forget it." Rafi sighed. "The pigs are already gone. The butcher said you never came. Since he didn't have the money, the kid that works for him sold Leni's pigs to someone else. Dom . . ." Rafi's voice wobbled. "El Señor Fuentes is pulling his hair out. He can't believe you didn't do what you promised."

Dom's stomach twisted into a monumental knot. "But I did. I gave the check to that boy! The one in the front office. His name is Vinnie. I had my musketeer hat on and he called me featherhead just like . . ."

"Dom?"

Dom's heart had stopped. Of course she knew that snarl. It was the Bublassi snarl. And that laugh. Ernie Bublassi laughed exactly like that. Ponsi Bublassi had called her "buckethead" when he'd tormented her during her knightly adventures. No wonder the boy at Tava's had looked familiar.

"Rafi." Dom was breathless. "I think that kid's a Bublassi. A dastardly Bublassi. Do you know someone named Vinnie Bublassi?"

Rafi's gasp joined the other two musketeers' gasps.

"Oh yes, I do!" Rafi said. "He's the oldest of the four Bublassis. And he works for Tava's Butcher. Rico, the Bublassi in my grade, brags that Vinnie brings free meat home all the time."

"Vinnie Bublassi tricked me! He took my check. And hid it. For some reason. I'll—I'll—I'll prove it. I'll prove that I handed him that check. And I'll get those pigs back. Don't you worry. El Señor Fuentes will still be able to put on the perfect party for Leni."

"Good luck, sis," her brother said. "But just in case, we're starting to make phone calls. We have to find more pigs by Saturday."

5
A Musketeer's Honor

Dom checked her plunger. The chocolate was dry. She tucked it into her baldric. "We must redeem my musketeer honor!"

Pancho and Steph nodded. The stumpy plumes in their hats bobbed as if to emphasize the trouble she was in. They picked up their plungers and followed her out the door.

"I need to get that receipt or that piece of paper,

whatever it was. And the check. So el Señor Fuentes will believe me. Then Mr. Tava will have to give el Señor Fuentes the pigs."

Steph put her hand out to stop Dom. "You can't just walk in there and ask Vinnie Bublassi to give you the receipt."

"Forsooth, why not?"

"The musketeer speaks the truth. We do not know Bublassi's dastardly reasons," Pancho said. "But he did it on purpose. And if he did it on purpose, he won't give it to you. Maybe he's even thrown it away already."

"Or maybe he ate it," Steph said. "I've heard of people doing that. Spies and all."

Pancho nodded as if he knew a Bublassi would be willing to eat a receipt.

"If he didn't eat it, I'll need to find it and get it back," Dom said.

"You can't steal it from the butcher shop!" Pancho protested.

Dom started walking again. "Stealing . . .

Stealing . . . Stealing is not a word I would choose, dearest friend. It's not stealing if what you take belonged to you to begin with."

Pancho didn't look so sure, and Steph stopped walking.

"You can't just give el Señor Fuentes a piece of paper, anyway," she said. "He could say you wrote the paper yourself. We need proof you got it from the drawer, right? We need to video you getting it."

"Yeah. And make sure it has a time stamp." Pancho recorded their knightly adventures with Dom's phone. He knew all about taking pictures. "You have to show it happened today and at what time it happened. I'll be your videographer."

They needed to get going. Any minute, Vinnie Bublassi could hide the receipt. Or eat it. They had to act quickly. But they also needed a plan. As they walked, they decided to ask the person behind the counter to check in the drawer. Fair and square. No pretending. Not at first. Of course, if they couldn't convince anyone to look in the drawer, then Pancho and Steph would distract the person while Dom raided the drawer.

"If Vinnie Bublassi's behind the counter, we may have to use our weapons."

"One for all and all for one!"

They hurried off to the butcher shop. Roco was gnawing on a bone and seemed happy to stay behind with Gran.

6
The Search for Evidence

The man towered over the counter. The peppery brush on his lip made his nose look huge. Mostly because it was huge. But the man also seemed neat. For a butcher. Because the tag on his apron said ANTONIO TAVA, and his apron sparkled. Not a drop of blood or guts on it.

Dom tried to be polite but firm, like a musketeer would be. "We're musketeers, and we're here to right a wrong. We're here to get the receipt I should have picked up earlier. At four twenty-two. Exactly. From Vinnie Bublassi."

Mr. Tava smiled, like he would at a cute baby. "And where would that receipt be?"

"In the drawer, but it may not be there anymore."

"And if it's not there anymore, how will I give it to you?"

"If it's not there anymore, it's somewhere else."

"And where would that be?"

"We need to ask Vinnie Bublassi. Maybe he ate it."

"You're the little girl who said you brought the check?"

Dom bristled. She did not like being called a little girl. Especially not now that she was a musketeer.

"I did bring the check. And I brought it on time. And Vinnie Bublassi took it, and he wrote a receipt. But he talked and talked and talked and made me angry so I would forget to pick up the receipt. Or else it would be in my hand right now and el Señor Fuentes could pick his pigs up in the morning"—she remembered to add some Musketeer to her speech— "forsooth."

"But Vinnie Bublassi said no one came from Fuentes with the check. And as far as the pigs . . ." Mr. Tava pulled out a receipt. "Uh . . . a Mr. Franklin Desmond took them home at four thirty-two."

"But Vinnie Bublassi's lying," Dom protested. "And if he's lying, he needs to go back and get the pigs from that Mr. Desmond guy."

"Why would Vinnie Bublassi lie? He got confused. He thought I said that if the check wasn't here, he should sell the pigs. Why would he sell the pigs to someone else?"

The only answer Dom could come up with was that she knew the Bublassis. They didn't need a reason to do something awful. She couldn't say that aloud, of course.

"That's what we need to find out," she said, putting an end to that side of the conversation for the moment. "For now, we need to find the check and the paper. At least we must prove to el Señor Fuentes that I did what he asked. My musketeer honor's at stake."

Mr. Tava shook his head.

Steph stepped up. "Kind sir, the musketeer's not

asking for much," she said. "It's her honor. She's looking for something that belongs to her. And she thinks she left it here. Could you please look in your drawer?"

Mr. Tava shook his head some more, but he invited Dom behind the counter.

"Come. Come see," he said, and he opened the drawer. "There's nothing here. No check here. No receipt."

The butcher was right. There was no check. And no receipt. *In* the drawer. But there was something *on* the drawer. Blood. Dom saw it on the hand the man pulled back in disgust. He wiped it on a towel that hung behind the counter.

"Excuse me, kind sir," Dom said. "Where is that blood from?"

"Uh, I'm not sure. Someone . . . someone . . ."

"I know exactly how that blood got there. I bet Vinnie Bublassi did it when he reached in to put away the check and write me the receipt. He smeared blood on the receipt. I saw him. Vinnie Bublassi got that blood on your drawer," Dom declared.

Steph stood up to the butcher. "And that means that what Musketeer Dom said is true. He wrote her the receipt. And we need to find it."

"If you don't mind," Pancho said. "I'll take a video while we look for the evidence."

"I don't think that's necessary." Mr. Tava bristled.

"But there is blood on your drawer. Someone must have put it there. You, at least, should let the musketeer search the butcher shop to see if she can clear her good name." Steph stood like a stone wall. "You know, a musketeer's good name is most important."

The butcher sighed. "Of course."

❧ ❧ ❧

It took seconds, not minutes, for Dom to find it. The crumpled, blood-smeared piece of paper. The one that said *Emilio Fuentes* and *Dominguita Melendez* and *3 suckling pigs* and *4:17* and *4:22*. And *PAID*. She found it in the trash can. Not on top, but not really hidden. Pancho took a picture of it while he filmed.

Now they had to find the check. They all knew that. Pancho continued taking videos while Steph and Dom looked. He took pictures of the calendar showing the day's date and followed it by focusing on his watch— just in case the time stamp on the video didn't work. He clicked to take stills while he took the videos.

But they didn't find anything. Not in the sales area.

"We need to keep looking," Steph said, heading toward a door with a glass window.

"Wait!" Mr. Tava stepped in front of them.

"We have proof that Vinnie, your person, wrote the receipt and threw it away. Now we need the check. It is totally necessary, you know." Steph tried to step around the butcher. "It's her honor at stake. We must clear her good name."

"Stop. I promise I'll help you clear your name. But you need to stay away from that door, please. That's where we cut the meat. It's bad enough you're in here with those filthy plungers. If bacteria infects the meat, I'll lose my store. I'll never be able to be a butcher again."

Dom nodded, but still she stepped toward the door. The others followed.

Through the glass on the top half of the door, they could see a second door—on the right—labeled REFRIGERATOR ROOM. It seemed to be a heavy metal door. On the left there were metal tables with cutting saws and scales. At a sink close to the door, a tall boy washed his hands.

"That's Vinnie!" Dom whispered as the boy reached for the paper towels. "I think . . . I think . . . I . . ."

The door opened, and Vinnie stepped into the salesroom.

"En poop!" Dom had been waiting all afternoon to do this. She stuck her plunger right under Vinnie's chin.

Steph pointed at one of Vinnie's ears.

Pancho at the other, while he kept filming.

Vinnie Bublassi raised his hands to hold them off, but he was cornered.

"Where did you put the check?"

Vinnie didn't answer.

Dom stepped closer to the door. Maybe that would get Mr. Tava to do something.

It worked.

"No, no, no." The butcher tried to stop her. "I beg you. Don't get any closer to the cutting room."

"Tell him to give you the check. We'll leave once the check is in our hands."

"VINNIE! DO YOU HAVE THE CHECK!"

"Okay, okay. I thought I was doing the right thing. Here's the check." Vinnie pulled it from his pocket and handed it to Mr. Tava. "I wasn't gonna cash it or nothin'."

The butcher let out the breath he'd been holding. It was a very long breath. "Thank you," he said.

Dom pulled back her plunger. She looked straight at Mr. Tava and dipped her index finger in her mouth to get it wet. She rubbed some brown stuff off the plunger and then licked it. "Yum."

"GROSS!" Vinnie Bublassi covered his mouth.

"DON'T!" Mr. Tava's face went very pale.

Steph presented her plunger to Mr. Tava as she pulled off a hard brown piece that was already peeling off. "Chocolate-covered plunger. Want a piece?"

Mr. Tava sighed. He shook his head and pointed his finger at Vinnie Bublassi.

"I didn't mean nothin' by it," the lying hyena said.

"Exactly," Dom said. "You didn't mean nothing. You meant something." She hated when people used double negatives incorrectly.

Antonio Tava snapped the receipt on his apron. "You had the money before four thirty and you still sold the pigs to someone else. You weren't confused at all. In fact, I get the feeling Mr. Desmond was just waiting for half past four to come get the pigs!"

The lying Bublassi shrugged. "I told you, I thought I was doing the right thing. What's the big deal? You could sell her chicken. Or we could pick up more pigs by tomorrow. Or maybe we can sell her some of the barbecue in the freezer. You'll make more money this way."

"That's not the point!" Mr. Tava snapped. "I promised Emilio Fuentes three suckling pigs for his granddaughter's quinceañera. He ordered them weeks ago."

The butcher shuffled back behind the counter. "I am so sorry," he told the musketeers.

Dom felt awful for the butcher. He had been Bublassied. Badly. But there was something she needed him to do. "Kind sir," she said quietly. "I need you to call el Señor Fuentes and clear my good name."

"I will call el Señor Fuentes and tell him you were here on time. You can show him the receipt as well. Then I'll try my best to find more pigs."

Dom bowed deeply, sweeping her musketeer hat to the ground. "I wish you the best of luck in finding those pigs. El Señor Fuentes is a good friend of the musketeers. And so is his granddaughter."

The butcher mopped his brow with a handkerchief and then pointed to Vinnie. "I don't know what got into him. But I will take care of all this."

Even though Dom's toes were doing a little dance because she'd revealed the dastardly deed, she wasn't totally happy. She needed more information.

"Kind merchant," she said. "Do you have an address or phone number for the Desmond gentleman? Mayhap having pigs, for him, is not as important as it is for the worthy Señor Fuentes's granddaughter."

"I already checked," the butcher said. "He paid with cash. Vinnie didn't take down a phone number or an address."

"Nope," Vinnie said. "Just a name."

Why was it that Dom saw a triumphant sneer in the hyena's eye?

7

An Unhappy Bublassi

The musketeers stopped at Dom's house to talk to Rafi. Dom waved the receipt in front of her brother's nose.

"See?" She pointed to the times on the paper. "I delivered the money on time."

Her brother shrugged. He was on his computer, searching the internet and writing notes on grid paper. "Sure, sure. You did the right thing. Great. But we still need to find three suckling pigs by tomorrow. No pigs, no quinceañera!"

"You mean you can't serve any other food?" Steph said. "It would make things easier."

Dom, Pancho, and Rafi all looked at one another.

Rafi tried to answer. "It's . . . tradition . . ."

"Cubans eat suckling pig for important holidays and parties, like Christmas and christenings and . . . quinceañeras," Pancho added.

"It's like most people eat turkey for Thanksgiving," Dom finished up. "It's tradition."

"The girl has a court of her friends, a little like bridesmaids. And they have special dances . . . ," Pancho added. "They cook the pigs in a special wooden box, using special spices. It really is tradition."

"Tradition . . ." Steph didn't seem too sure.

"Anyway, we need to worry about a lot of other things. Not just the pigs. Vinnie Bublassi's up to something," Dom said. "You should have seen the smirk on his face when Mr. Tava told us there was no way to call the Desmond man who bought the pigs."

"Mr. Tava said it was a mistake." Rafi was still scrolling on his computer.

"He changed his mind by the time we left." Dom tried to get her brother to pay attention to them. "The thing is, why would a guy show up and buy three suckling pigs just like that?"

"Yeah." Rafi stopped his scrolling to agree. "They're expensive. And hard to get. You wouldn't just show up and buy them."

For a couple of seconds there was total silence in Rafi's room.

"Okay," Dom said. "It's pretty strange that he just showed up and bought the pigs right at half past four without ordering them or anything. We can agree to that."

"Right," Pancho said. "So that tells me we're pretty sure Vinnie Bublassi and this Franklin Desmond are in cahoots."

"It does," Steph agreed. "They're in cahoots."

Rafi shook his head. "I know you guys want some grand conspiracy so you can be musketeers, but you don't do something like that without a good reason."

"Vinnie Bublassi's trying to mess up Leni's party.

He doesn't need a reason. Bublassis never need a reason to be nasty," Dom said. "And that Desmond guy is helping him."

Steph waved her hands. "Maybe Leni did something to make Vinnie Bublassi angry . . . or hurt his feelings. And that Desmond guy is helping him get back at her. When you want revenge, you don't care about money," she said.

Rafi turned around slowly. "You know, Musketeer Steph? You may be right on the revenge part. But it wasn't Leni. She isn't even Vinnie's friend—he's a senior. Vinnie worked for el Señor Fuentes about three months ago. But Leni told me he only lasted a couple of days. He was always late and always talking on the phone, so Señor Fuentes fired him."

"Ooh!"

"Yeah! It gets worse," Rafi said. "His mother found out and grounded him. He missed a football practice and he didn't get to play in the homecoming game. It was all over the school."

"Now, that's a good reason for revenge!" Pancho raised his plunger.

"Bublassi's trying to get back at Señor Fuentes for sure!" Dom jumped on Rafi's bed and raised hers.

"I'll go along with that." Steph's plunger met the other two. A shower of chocolate followed the collision.

"Aw, man! Get off my bed!" Rafi brushed the broken chocolate slivers off his bed and into his hand. "Look what you did!"

"Sorry, sorry, sorry!" Dom jumped down and helped her brother, taking a bite or two as she picked up the pieces.

"Wait, wait, wait," Steph didn't care at all about the chocolate. "Is it really musketeery? I get it about revenge, but I thought *The Three Musketeers* was about somebody in love and someone else tries to mess it up! Nobody's in love here."

Dom wasn't about to give up her idea. "There was a lot of revenge in *The Three Musketeers*!" she said.

"Vinnie Bublassi wants revenge on the grandfather, and he finds a way to do it through Leni's party!" That was Pancho.

"Exactly." Dom raised her arms in triumph.

"Vinnie Bublassi finds out the pigs are for Leni's party. For her biggest party ever: her quinceañera. He's already trying to figure out how to mess things up when I show up with the check. Selling the pigs for a quinceañera to someone else? The best way to take revenge."

"On top of that"—Pancho held up a finger—"when we were knights, we made Ernie and Ponsi Bublassi look bad. Now, with the pig caper, Vinnie Bublassi made Dom look bad—Bublassi revenge for the knightly adventure. Exactly like the musketeers!"

"We have to stop the Bublassis!"

"We have to help Leni and el Señor Fuentes!"

"For el Señor Fuentes and for Leni!" As Dom raised her plunger again, she almost knocked down one of Rafi's baseball trophies.

"Whoa, whoa!" Rafi said. "Calm down."

"We can't calm down!" Pancho said. "He could be trying to ruin everything about Leni's party, and the pigs are just the beginning."

"Look, guys," Rafi said. "All this musketeer stuff is fun, but I don't have time to play."

49

"But the other stuff, Rafi. The other party stuff. What if they try to mess with anything else?"

"You guys check on what else Vinnie Bublassi could do." Rafi started clicking on his computer again. "That will be great. And don't forget to take lots of pictures and really good notes. I don't have time to do any writing for Abuela right now. I need to call these shops before they close. No pigs, no party."

"But, Rafi," Dom said. "We need to talk to Leni. We need to find out what else Vinnie Bublassi could mess up!"

Rafi turned around, his eyes flashing. "NO WAY!" he yelled. "Her grandfather doesn't want her worried. Whatever you want to do, do it yourself."

🌿 🌿 🌿

"Forsooth," Musketeer Pancho said in the elevator. "Rafi's trying so hard to find pigs for the party, he can't think about what else Vinnie Bublassi could do. He doesn't think the dastardly one will strike again."

"But Vinnie won't give up with just the pigs," Dom said. "The Bublassis never give up on dastardliness."

"And musketeers help whoever's helped them, like el Señor Fuentes," Pancho said.

"And musketeers figure out what they have to do," Steph added.

"So we will stop Vinnie Bublassi from making things worse." Dom stepped out and stood at the corner of her building. She put her sword out. "Stop the Bublassis!"

Pancho and Steph crossed their swords with hers. "Stop the Bublassis!"

They asked a passerby to take a picture. Most of the chocolate had already fallen off the plungers and they weren't gross at all.

Sword back in her baldric, Musketeer Dom spoke first.

"And how do we stop them? What's our next step?"

"Why don't you call your abuela," Steph suggested. "It won't take long. And she might remember her quinceañera. Maybe she can tell us what Leni needs.

After school tomorrow, we can try to keep the dastardly Bublassis from ruining the party."

It was a brilliant idea.

If Abuela could remember her quinceañera.

But she didn't always remember.

That's why she was living with her sister in Florida now. Instead of in Mundytown with Dom and Rafi.

Musketeer Dom crossed her fingers and called Abuela. She put the call on speakerphone.

"Hola, mi amor. I'm so glad to hear your voice. I was rereading your pirate adventures. You and your friends were brave!"

Yes! Dom winked at the other musketeers. Abuela seemed fine today!

"We're musketeers now, Abuela. On a new adventure. Trying to help el Señor Fuentes." Dom quickly explained what had happened so far. "So I need you to tell me about your quinceañera party. We need to figure out where else Vinnie Bublassi can stick his nose."

"Oh my goodness, mi amor," Abuela said. "I never had one."

"What do you mean, Abuela?"

"It takes money for a big party like that. We left all we owned in Cuba. We were so poor when we first came to the United States, we didn't have furniture. Or a phone. I slept on a mattress on the floor. My sisters and I never had a real birthday party after we came from Cuba. I definitely never had a quinceañera!"

Dom remembered what el Señor Fuentes had said. He wanted Leni's party to be perfect because her grandmother didn't have a quinceañera and he couldn't afford one for Leni's mother. Dom had never thought about how things were when her grandmother and other Cubans first came to the United States. She felt lucky she'd never had to.

Abuela was still going strong. She could remember things that happened a long time ago. "I think for that birthday my parents gave me a tube of lipstick and some pantyhose—you know, see-through tights. I felt very lucky they gave me that."

"Oh," Dom said.

"Don't worry, though," Abuela said. "My sister Yuyú was older. She had one a couple of months before we left Cuba."

Abuela talked about flowers and cakes. Appetizers to pass around. Main courses and side dishes. Drinks for adults and drinks for the kids. Plates and silverware and tablecloths and napkins. "And I bet you Leni gets a nice piece of jewelry," Abuela ended. "Yuyú did, a pearl necklace, but she had to leave it."

That was a lot of good information. But Abuela wasn't done. "So what did you say your problem was?"

"This guy. He's trying to ruin the party. We think he's upset because Leni's grandfather got him in trouble."

"Exactly!" Abuela said. "I knew there was something I wanted to say about that. I remember a boy was upset Yuyú didn't pick him to be her escort, and he was a pain at the party. Sometimes an unhappy boy can ruin a party."

Abuela was saying the same thing they'd been trying to tell Rafi! Even if her brother was too busy to think about it, Abuela agreed with them!

"Oh, Abuela. Gracias! Mil *gracias*! You are the best. I'll let you know what happens. And I'm sure Rafi will write a book about our musketeer adventures for you. With many, many pictures!"

"You are the best too, ah . . . ah . . . musketeer. And tell that boy, that boy . . ."

Dom could hear Abuela start to drift. "Rafi."

"Tell Rafi I love him. I can't wait to read his next book."

8
The Dastardly Plans

Friday afternoon, after school, Dom stuffed her musketeer sword into her baldric. She and Pancho met at Steph's house. They were ready to try to make sure Leni's party went off without a hitch.

"Bakery," Pancho said. "Your Abuela talked about a cake. So we need to check the bakery. There's only one in Mundytown—three blocks from here."

"And if we find out Vinnie Bublassi messed up the cake order, Rafi will believe us."

"If we find out Vinnie Bublassi messed this up too, *everyone* will listen to us."

A few minutes later, they rounded a corner, and Pancho pointed to a sign across the street: SWEET TOOTH BAKERY. The three musketeers crossed over.

❧ ❧ ❧

When they entered the bakery, the smell of delicious, fresh-baked cakes and icing made their heads swim. The baker was on the phone. "Yes, Mr. Desmond. The cake will be ready by nine a.m. on Saturday."

The three musketeers gasped at what they heard, but they recovered by the time the baker hung up.

"Kind lady," Pancho said when the woman turned to face them. "Was that excellent Desmond fellow named Frank? Frank Desmond?"

The woman scrunched her forehead. "How did you know?"

"Forsooth, there may be a problem," Dom said.

"Forsooth?"

"Forsooth. We are musketeers, and Mr. Desmond is related to problems with Leni Fuentes's quinceañera party."

"Related?" Now the woman was beginning to look annoyed.

"Strange things are happening," Steph said. "Like Leni Fuentes's pigs being sold to Franklin Desmond when they shouldn't be. By Vinnie Bublassi. Connected, right? Related?"

The baker narrowed her eyes.

"That excellent fellow Desmond didn't perchance try to take Leni's cake, did he? Like he took the pigs?" Dom said.

"Wait, wait. Why would he? And how did you know Leni ordered her cake from me?"

"Kind lady, think of it," Pancho said. "You are the only baker in Mundytown. A very good reason for Leni to order her cake from you. Forsooth, that was what brought us musketeers here."

"Oh." The baker still didn't seem sure she should be wasting her time with the musketeers. "Mr. Desmond told me Leni had given him my

name. Why would he do that if he wants to mess up her order?"

"Mayhap that's why he said that she gave him your name," Dom said. "To make sure. To make sure you were doing Leni's cake. And . . ."

"Let dastardly Vinnie Bublassi strike again!"

"Bublassi? You were talking about Desmond!" The baker picked up her paperwork. "Really.

Playing musketeers is fun and all. I get it. But there's no mystery here. He just placed an order for a sheet cake. Why don't you go play musketeers somewhere else?"

"We can see that you are distressed, kind lady—most kind lady. But we are trying to stop you from making a terrible mistake. If a mistake can be made."

"A disastrous mistake."

"A colossal mistake."

"If a mistake can be made."

The woman frowned and started to come out from behind the counter.

"So we will leave," Dom said. "And hold council outside. But not before we leave you with our calling card." Dom tore a sheet of paper from her notebook and wrote her number next to the word "musketeer."

"If anything happens, you know where to reach us."

The musketeers scurried out of the bakery.

They paused at a bench on the sidewalk outside the bakery. Sort of hidden under the canopy of a very weepy tree. They chose it in case a Bublassi decided to stalk them.

"We need to figure out the connection between Frank Desmond and Vinnie Bublassi," Pancho said.

"This Desmond person. He's having a party," Dom said. "But not a quinceañera. If it was a quinceañera, the invitations would have been out weeks ago. He wouldn't buy the pigs and order the cake two days before. Not for a quinceañera."

Pancho agreed. "Forsooth, I see that."

"Musketeer Dom, please get your paper out," Steph said. "What do we know? What do we need to know? That's how we can find the connection between Desmond and Bublassi."

"Right," Pancho said. This was a trick the crew used to solve problems. "Get the paper out."

Dom put the notebook on top of her bag. "So what *do* we know?"

"Can we say we know that Bublassi and Desmond are related?"

"They have to be," Dom said. "At least they're in cahoots."

"We'll know for sure if something happens to Leni's cake order," Pancho said.

Before Dom could write that down, they heard the bakery's door opening.

Pancho turned. "Mayhap we're about to find out right now."

The baker crooked her finger and motioned for the musketeers to come back.

"Well," she said when they stepped inside. "You musketeers were right."

"You mean a mistake could have been made but you didn't make it?" Dom asked.

"Something like that. Right as you left, someone called and tried to change what Leni ordered. Imagine! The person who called wanted me to make cupcakes decorated like basketballs instead of a cake with three tiers and a beautiful quinceañera doll on top. She wanted me to change the topper to say 'Queen of the Court.'"

"So . . . what did you do?"

"I said of course," the bakery woman said. "What else could I say? But that doesn't mean I'll do anything."

"You saved the day, kind lady," Pancho said. "By not doing anything."

"I did call Leni, though. I said I wanted to double-check the order." The woman shook her head. "Leni had no clue."

"Do you know who called, kind lady?" Pancho finally asked. "Was it a maiden or a crone? A young lad or an old man?"

"Sounded like a maiden, of course. But a false maiden. She said she was Leni, but I didn't recognize the voice. And it cracked. More like a boy—uh, lad—pretending to be a maiden. Thank goodness for what you told me. I would have definitely made a mistake if you hadn't. A huge mistake."

"Colossal crisis contained!" Dom yelled. She wanted to pull out her plunger in salute, but she didn't want to give the baker a heart attack. Instead, she high-fived all around.

"If you'll forgive us," Steph said. "We must be going. We must try to stop a fantastical fiasco at the florist."

Pancho turned back at the door. "You don't mayhap know the name of a florist where Leni would have gone?"

"I know exactly where she went! Mundytown Blooms. Leni told me the owner's daughter is her friend. I know the woman. I think her daughter's name is Emily."

They were armed with abundant amounts of amazing information.

"Away!" Dom said. "First a selfie and then to Mundytown Blooms!"

❧ ❧ ❧

At Mundytown Blooms, Dom cleared her throat to get the florist's attention. "Ahem. We're three musketeers and we're on a mission."

The woman raised her eyebrows. "Musketeers..."

"We're here to make sure a fantastical misfortune doesn't flourish at your florist," Pancho added.

"A fantastical misfortune?" The florist leaned over the counter.

"A definitive disaster," Steph clarified, "that could ruin Leni Fuentes's quinceañera party."

"Leni Fuentes?" Now the woman behind the counter was as annoyed as the baker. "This is the third time someone has asked about Leni Fuentes in"—she looked at her watch—"the last ten minutes."

"Let me guess," Pancho said. "An excellent gent named Frank Desmond called to place an order. He said that Leni Fuentes had told him to call you."

The woman gave them a surprised look.

Pancho continued. "Then a young maiden with a cracking voice called to change the order for Leni Fuentes's party. Am I close now? Lady? Kind lady?"

"Yes!" the woman exclaimed. "It was definitely a cracking voice. She said she was Leni, but I didn't recognize the voice." The woman jutted out her chin. "And how did you know all that?"

"Forsooth," Pancho said. "It's happened before!"

"And what did you do about it . . . *before*?"

"We prevented the villain from ruining Leni's party."

"And what did *you* do . . . this time?" Dom asked the florist.

"Absolutely nothing," the woman said. "Not yet. It will cost me a lot to make the change."

"You could check with Leni," Dom said. "Just ask to go over the order. That way you'll know if she really wants to make a change . . . without worrying her if she didn't."

"Right!" The florist pulled up Leni's order in the computer and began punching in numbers. As she did, her eyes widened. She looked up at the musketeers, but before she could say anything, Leni had answered. Quickly, the florist confirmed the order for blue and purple wildflowers and hung up with a big sigh.

"A cataclysmic catastrophe circumvented?" Steph asked, and began to give high fives all around.

"No, no, Musketeers," the lady said. "I just noticed something fishy." She showed them her cell phone screen. "The last one is Leni's number. Look at the two calls before."

"Holy plungers!" Pancho said. "They're the same!"

"One of them is Desmond and the other one is the pretend Leni?" Dom asked.

The florist nodded. "Exactly. Two different people called from the same phone. Within minutes of each other. The first was a man who said he was Desmond. The other was the crackly girlish voice who said she was Leni."

"Oh, kind lady," Pancho said. "The quinceañera conspiracy continues!"

"And we have to stop it!" Steph added.

"Is there anything that you know that could help us, lady? Kind lady?"

The florist scrunched her forehead and peered into the eyes of the three musketeers, one at a time. "The plot may be bigger than you think, Musketeers. When Desmond placed his order, he asked when I would deliver Leni's flowers, or if she was coming to pick them up. He wants to pick up his flowers at the same time."

"And what time would that be?"

"Twelve thirty tomorrow," the florist said. "Good luck!"

❧ ❧ ❧

"We must come back at twelve thirty tomorrow and make sure they don't succeed!" Pancho said once they closed the door behind them.

"We'll come back to the florist to make sure the flowers get to Leni's party," Steph said.

Dom punched the air. "Leni's party will not be ruined."

They gave one another the musketeer salute, took a selfie, and walked on to prevent further dastardly disasters.

9
The Proof

"That's the proof we've been waiting for!" Dom said as they crossed the first street.

"Whoever's changing Leni's order is in cahoots with Franklin Desmond."

"Vinnie Bublassi!" Steph said. "And I think that crackly voiced maiden is either Ernie or Ponsi. You can't get more dastardly than that!"

"No," Pancho said. "*We* know it's Vinnie Bublassi. And he probably made Ernie or Ponsi help him with the phone calls. But we can't say for sure. We don't have any proof."

"At least we can tell Rafi. He has to believe us now." She took out her phone to call her brother. He and Mr. Tava's son had left after school to pick up two pigs in Pennsylvania.

The phone rang before Dom had time to punch in his number. It was Rafi. She put him on speakerphone.

"Finally," he said. "I couldn't get through to you. Someone's trying to mess with more than the pigs!"

Dom and the musketeers could have said *I told you so*, but this was not the time.

"Look," he said. "Reception here is awful. Just let me tell you what you need to do. Ben Gonzales, from Kowalski's, was about to take the food for the party to Yuca, Yuca so el Señor Prieto can cook it all tomorrow. And two boys showed up about thirty minutes ago. They're just hanging around. And waiting. I'm afraid they're Bublassis. I think when Ben leaves the building with the food, they'll try something."

The musketeers gasped.

"Forsooth, you speak the truth. Ernie and Ponsi for sure!" Dom said.

"And they're waiting for Vinnie," Steph added.

"We can't say—" Pancho began, but both girls stared him down.

"Send them on a wild-goose chase," Rafi said. "Talk—B—Gonzales—figure—out."

"Got it," Dom said, even though she hadn't heard any of the last part of what her brother had said.

A "call failed" notice came up on her screen.

"My uncle's picking up the third pig in North Carolina," Pancho said. "It's totally up to us!"

"Well, then," Dom said. "Musketeers to the rescue!"

They planned as they walked, stopping at Steph's house for a prop. Roco was still in her kitchen. He didn't seem to have anything better to do, so he followed them.

❧ ❧ ❧

As they neared the grocery store, they called Ben Gonzales. The night watchman at Kowalski's was another friend. They had met him during their pirate adventure. Because he'd found Kowalski's treasure, the grocery store owner let him live in the apartment over the grocery store for free. During the day, he was the janitor at a building by Monroe Park. In the evenings, he kept an eye on Kowalski's security cameras and responded to any alarms. The musketeers had one big question.

"Ben," Dom said into the phone. "Where are those boys?"

"In alley." Ben's English was a bit chopped.

"We'll come through the front, then, and meet you inside the store," Pancho said. From the alley, the Bublassis wouldn't see them approach or go in through the front door. Roco would be able to stay cool in the shade of the awning.

"Pirates look like . . . ," Ben said when they met.

"Musketeers," Dom said. "We're musketeers now, Ben."

"So who Porthos and Aramis and Athos and D'Artagnan?" Ben knew the classics like *Treasure Island* and *The Three Musketeers* backward and forward. "I get it. Rafi's D'Artagnan."

Dom high-fived the man in overalls. "Ahh, we didn't take on the names of the musketeers, Ben. Things started happening too quickly. And you're right. Rafi probably is D'Artagnan. And he sent us to help you. Did you call him?"

"I call him," the man in overalls said. "Mr. Kowalski in New York. He say call Yuca, Yuca. Woman at Yuca, Yuca say call Rafi about party stuff."

Ben Gonzales told them he'd noticed two boys circling the store. He showed them the current video and fast-forwarded through video of the last hour or so.

"It's the Bublassis all right!" Steph said. "Ernie and Ponsi, for sure."

Around back. Around the front. Ben was afraid they'd try to stop him if he tried to take the food to Yuca, Yuca. The musketeers agreed.

"Why they around here and around here if they good boys?" Ben said.

The musketeers couldn't answer that, but they had a plan.

"Ben," Dom said. "You know where the ice-cream

cart is? The one Mr. Kowalski uses on really hot days to sell ice cream outside?"

Ben nodded. "By cash register. You need wheels?"

Dom knew exactly what he meant. When Rafi worked for Mr. Kowalski, he sometimes manned the ice-cream cart. He had to bring down the wheels to be able to roll it outside. "We need wheels. Let's go."

They worked quickly. Without much talking. Ben and Steph emptied the ice-cream cart and pulled down the wheels. Dom and Pancho hurried to the store's back room to pick up the boxes for the party. Some from a freezer and others from a fridge. They carried them to the cart.

They filled the bottom of the cart with the party food. Then they piled on as much ice-cream as they could. They ended up with three layers of prewrapped ice cream—cones, sandwiches, and Popsicles—over the party food. The ice cream that didn't fit, they stowed in the back freezer.

They told Ben their plan, and before they left, the three musketeers did a plunger salute. "All for one," they said, because, in truth, they were all working to make Leni's party perfect. They got Ben to take a picture.

❧ ❧ ❧

Steph lost Rock Paper Scissors, so she pushed the cart. Dom and Pancho escorted her. Roco brought up the rear. The procession proceeded, feathers waving, plungers rocking, and Roco's tail wagging as they walked. The four paraded down the sidewalk toward Yuca, Yuca—it would be a six-block walk. Ben followed them at a distance.

At first the Bublassis didn't show. Which was a good thing.

If they got to Yuca, Yuca without any Bublassi sightings, they would be happy.

But that didn't happen. When they crossed the first street, the Bublassis saw them. A block and a half away from Kowalski's, the two younger Bublassis were already behind them.

"Ernie!" Pancho said, looking back.

"Ponsi!" Steph greeted the bully like a long-lost buddy. "My good man!"

The Bublassis drew even with the musketeers at the end of the block. They all crossed the street.

"Are you perchance on the search for cold refreshment?" Dom said. "We have an abundance in this carriage."

"She means ice cream," Pancho translated, still walking. "The cart is full of it."

Ponsi looked doubtful.

Three and a half blocks to go.

"We're taking this cart to Yuca, Yuca for an ice cream giveaway," Steph said without slowing down. She glanced at the other musketeers as if she needed their permission. "Methinks the kind owner of Yuca, Yuca would be happy to share his bounty." She opened the top of the freezer cart, showing off the icy treats.

Ponsi didn't reach in, but Ernie eyed the wrapped cones and licked his lips.

All three musketeers crossed their fingers that Ernie and Ponsi wouldn't want to dig deep.

Still walking, Dom picked out a fudge-drizzled

vanilla ice cream from the top layer and handed it to Ernie. "Be our guest. Don't be shy."

"It's free," Pancho said. "You don't have to pay anything. All you can eat." And to prove his point, he opened an orange Popsicle for Roco, who slurped it quickly.

Dom reached for another ice cream and handed it to Ponsi. "You could come by Yuca, Yuca and have more later. We'll be setting up as soon as we get there."

"All you can eat," Pancho repeated.

They were now four blocks from Kowalski's and two blocks from Yuca, Yuca. Ponsi, tearing the wrapper of his ice cream open, looked undecided. Like half of him wanted to stay and gorge himself on ice cream and the other half wanted to rush away to do whatever dastardly deed he needed to do at Kowalski's.

"I don't blame you for being of two minds, dear man," Pancho said. "We musketeers are of two minds as well. We would love to stay and partake of the food and merriment at Yuca, Yuca, but we must away to L'Hotel de Ville in Tuddytown to pick up precious cargo for tomorrow's celebration."

The Bublassis stopped, and for the first time since they left Kowalski's, so did the musketeers.

"Wha—wha—what was that you said?"

"Mayhap you did not understand." Steph reached down to pat Roco. "We will be journeying forthwith to L'Hotel de Ville, a most excellent establishment. There, we will pick up the victuals for tomorrow's celebration."

"She means food for Leni Fuentes's party," Pancho translated.

"Not—not—not Kowalski's?"

"Oh no, my dear man." Dom put her hand on Ponsi's back and led him away like a conspirator. Then she crossed her fingers again. She was about to tell a whopper. "Kowalski's is not a worthy establishment. The young maiden did not order her food from Kowalski's."

"Nay, nay!" Pancho told Ponsi, crossing his fingers too. "Yuca, Yuca doesn't buy anything from Kowalski's anymore. L'Hotel de Ville is the place. Tuddytown. Straight down Twenty-Seventh. I've picked up victuals for my uncle there many times."

Ponsi didn't look convinced, but he and Ernie

went along. Only a block away. The musketeers had been lucky.

But their luck was about to run out.

"What is it you have in here?" Ponsi pointed to the cart.

"Ice cream, of course," Steph said. "You saw it yourself. Would you like to take a deeper look?"

"Ah, well, yes," Pancho said. "If you would like, you may do so when we reach yon establishment." He pointed to Yuca, Yuca. "But right now, as we walk, we should obtain the route to our next assignation. You know we must away quickly. You're welcome to stay at Yuca, Yuca and examine the contents after we've left."

"Ah yes." Dom sighed. "I do wish we could stay and partake of the cold refreshment. But a musketeer's duty is never done." She pulled out a piece of paper from her bag with great secrecy. They had typed it up and printed it out at Steph's house. It read L'HOTEL DE VILLE across the top in huge letters. In less huge letters was the address: 221B Baker Street. Below was a list of foods likely to be bought for a party, like carrot sticks, cheese cubes, and cucumber sandwiches.

Ponsi looked over her shoulder.

Dom turned to him and scorched him with her eyes. She folded the piece of paper quickly. "I fear, kind sir," she said, "that you spy on me without shame."

"At least you could have shame," Steph said.

"Or even better," Pancho added. "Forget the spying."

Dom said the address under her breath, but loud enough for everyone to hear, and then punched it into her phone's GPS. In trying to hide it from Ponsi, she showed it to Ernie. She could see the younger Bublassi mouthing the address. *221B Baker Street. 221B Baker Street.*

Almost to Yuca, Yuca, Steph made her last offer. "May I interest you in another cold refreshment for the road?"

"Or will you be staying at Yuca, Yuca to continue to partake?" Dom added.

"We're going!" Ponsi said.

"It won't hurt us to take one for the road," Ernie whined.

"With our compliments," Pancho said. He reached for two more ice creams and handed them to the villains. "And now we must deliver this carriage into the establishment and away to our next assignation."

The musketeers pushed the cart through the door into the restaurant's refrigerated room before they crumpled to the floor laughing.

When they calmed down, they gave themselves a plunger salute. Then they asked one of the cooks to take a picture of them next to the cart. They deserved it. They had brought the food to Yuca, Yuca safely. They unloaded the ice-cream cart and checked in with Ben. No Bublassis anywhere he could see.

"We're not done, though," Pancho said after they texted Rafi the picture. "This stuff is safe. It's what my uncle's cooking at Yuca, Yuca tomorrow. But since Rafi's not here and my uncle's still out picking up Leni's third pig, we have to figure out how to protect the cake, the flowers, and everything else. The party's at the community center, and all that stuff has to get there tomorrow. Disasters could still happen."

"And catastrophes."

"And just plain messes."

The Musketeer Plans

Steph's gran wanted her home, so the musketeers and Roco moved on to her house for pizza.

They planned and plotted. And plotted and planned.

They reached the baker by phone. She agreed with their plan and promised to make a pretend topper for Leni's "cake." The musketeers made cupcakes and iced them. Orange. With black curvy lines—like basketballs. Gran would pick up the real cake at the back door while the musketeers distracted the dastardly Bublassis at the front.

Next was the florist. She still agreed there was a conspiracy to ruin the quinceañera but didn't want the musketeers' help. She said her daughter, Emily, convinced her she shouldn't worry about Vinnie Bublassi.

Even though the musketeers didn't like that answer, they had to accept the florist's wishes. For now. They thought of different ways to stop any Bublassi plans to ruin the flower delivery, but none of them was spectacular. They decided to figure it out in the morning.

In between the planning, cupcake making, and eating pepperoni pizza with Gran's chocolate chip cookies for dessert, they made a chart of everything they would do the next day. They didn't leave out one thing. They took a picture of the chart to keep on Dom's phone. Since they had to be up so early, Dom and Roco spent the night. Pancho only lived two blocks over.

❧ ❧ ❧

At six the next morning, the musketeers delivered the basketball cupcakes to the baker. They would be back to pick them up at nine—at the same time Desmond was scheduled to pick up his cake.

And they were. They stood outside the bakery making so much noise that Ponsi Bublassi, who was there waiting for them, knew for sure that the musketeers had arrived. Desmond was nowhere to be seen, but that was not a problem.

At 9:07 the three musketeers left the bakery

each carrying a box. Two boxes held the basketball cupcakes they'd made the night before. The third box held a pretend cake topper the baker had made to really fool the Bublassis. It said "Leni, Queen of the Court" around a basketball jersey with the number fifteen on it. It was perfect.

Ponsi showed up next to them as if by magic. Ernie was a few steps behind him.

Ponsi's foot stuck out in a perfect position to trip Dom. "Whatcha got there, loser-keteers?"

Dom was sure the Bublassis wanted to see if the order had been changed. If not, they would mess it up. "Sweets for a maiden's party," she answered.

"We are the carriers," Steph added.

"Speedy delivery," Pancho finished. "Forsooth!"

"Although mayhap I wouldn't like this type of sweet for my festivities," Dom said, and lifted the top of her box without being asked.

The other two musketeers did the same.

"The maiden has unique taste," Dom said. "Wouldn't you agree? Actually, I think I'd like a picture of this. Do you mind?" Dom handed her phone to Ernie, and the three musketeers posed along with Roco.

It was easy to see that Ernie and Ponsi were having a really hard time not rolling on the sidewalk laughing. They could see that dastardly Vinnie had gotten his way! Ernie took the picture. Which took a long time. Because each of the musketeers had to fix the feathers on his or her hat. Slowly. One at a time.

Which gave even more time for Gran's minivan to speed away from the back door of the bakery with the real cake. The musketeers needed to keep the two bullies with them for a bit longer. To give Gran the time to reach the community center.

"We're dropping this off at Musketeer Steph's house," Dom said to Ponsi. "You know where that is, right?" The reason Steph was one of the musketeers was that Dom and Pancho had rescued her from Ponsi's pestering.

Ponsi grunted.

"Her Gran is taking us to L'Hotel de Ville to pick up the order we told you about yesterday," Pancho said. "Wanna come? We could use the help."

"There's no such place!" Ponsi yelled. "We looked and looked but couldn't—"

"You looked!" Dom's eyes said *Gotcha!*

"No, no," Ernie said. "We didn't go nowhere."

"That means that you went somewhere, my man. Why would you be visiting that far place?" Dom said.

"Mayhap you should come with us now and we'll show you where it is," Steph said.

"We have better things to do," Ernie said.

"There's no way you'll be able to stop everything we've planned to ruin your little party," Ponsi added.

"Oh, we're so worried." Dom pretended to shiver.

"Have fun!" Pancho added.

"Spend all the time you want," Steph finished.

❧ ❧ ❧

Gran texted to say the cake arrived safely at the community center. All of Leni's food, including three suckling pigs, picked up the day before, was safe and cooking at Yuca, Yuca. The dastardly ones couldn't do any damage there. The musketeers also knew that

Ernie and Ponsi were both braggarts, so they would say they had big plans just to scare them.

But still.

The brothers said they had plans. . . .

Which sent shivers through the musketeers' spines.

But Franklin Desmond was about to be at Mundytown Blooms. An hour and a half after that, the florist would deliver Leni's flowers to the community center.

Since the florist didn't want the musketeers to help her, they were still unsure what to do when they reached her shop. Especially Musketeer Steph.

"We should not do things on our own," Steph said.

"But we proved Desmond's in cahoots with the dastardly Bublassis," Pancho said.

"And they have *big plans*!" Dom added.

"But still." Steph wasn't so sure. "She's the owner. We should do what she wants."

Dom knew she had to make the decision. "When Leni's flowers end up in pieces on the sidewalk, we'll be wishing we'd tried. We talk to Desmond. If nothing happens, then we hope the florist is right. But we must try."

❧ ❧ ❧

They waited on the bench outside the florist, and when they saw a man park his car and head toward the florist's door, they doffed their hats and bowed low in greeting.

"Forgive me, kind sir," Pancho said. "But would you be the honorable Franklin Desmond?"

The man nodded with a *how-did-you-know* look in his eyes.

"Certain happenings have been happening, kind sir," Steph explained. "That are far from being nice happenings. Very, very far."

"You may be involved in a dastardly plot even if you don't know it," Dom explained.

Desmond wouldn't let himself be confused. "But if I don't know it, why would it matter?"

"Because you can stop it. Even if you don't know

it. If the dastardly plan succeeds, a quinceañera party will be ruined."

"But how am I involved, and how can I stop it if I don't know?"

"Your phone, kind sir." Pancho pointed to the man's phone, which they could all see in his pocket. "Your phone is at fault."

"The Bublassi brothers commandeered it." Dom knew this was the moment of truth. "You know the Bublassi brothers, of course."

Desmond was slow to admit it. "I do," he finally said. "But what of it?"

"You know them well!" Dom pressed.

Desmond took a few seconds to answer. As if he was afraid of what the musketeers would tell him.

"Their mother's my partner," he said slowly. "We live in the same house. Why do you want to know?"

"Kind sir, let me tell you what's what."

❧ ❧ ❧

"I see," Franklin Desmond said when the musketeers finished their story.

All three musketeers waited. They couldn't even breathe.

"And what would you like me to do? She's my partner, but they're not my children."

"You could call a council," Dom suggested.

"Today," Steph added.

"Now," Pancho said.

"And keep them away until the florist delivers the flowers," Dom said. "Later if possible. They plan to ruin the quinceañera!"

"Don't you know a tower where you could keep all of them together until the party's over?" Pancho wondered.

"A tower?" Desmond asked, his eyebrows arched.

"A colossally high tower. Out in the country would be perfect." In *The Three Musketeers*, the villain had been jailed in a tower for days and days to prevent her from hurting the queen.

"I'll tell you what I'll do." Desmond grabbed the door handle. "I'll talk to the florist. If what you said is true, I'll call them. Right here. In front of you. And ask them to meet me and their mother."

"And later?"

"We'll see," the man said, and he went through the door.

Five minutes later, Desmond came out of the florist balancing two large vases of flowers. He stowed them in his car and beckoned the musketeers. He punched in a number, and through the speakerphone, Vinnie Bublassi answered.

"I need all of you to meet your mother and me at my warehouse at twelve thirty. We need your help with the party."

There was silence at the other end of the line.

"Vinnie, your mother's already meeting me. I need your help."

"I told you I had an appointment. And all of us can't come. Rico's working."

"Okay. Rico's excused. But I'm telling you I need you."

The musketeers could hear an annoyed sigh from the other side of the phone. "Okay, okay. My

93

appointment's in half an hour," Vinnie said. "Ernie and Ponsi are helping me. But we should be able to make it by twelve thirty."

"Fine," Desmond said. "I'll see you then."

Desmond turned to the musketeers. "It's the best I can do. They have to leave before twelve thirty to get to my warehouse. The flower delivery should be safe. I'll keep them busy after that with my party. That should take care of everything you need, right?"

Dom barely nodded. She was trying to work things out in her head. What appointment? Vinnie Bublassi must be planning to ruin something else.

"Kind sir," she said. "Would you mayhap know what the appointment might be?"

"I heard him talking about a jewelry store," Desmond said. "Probably getting a present for his mother or something. Her birthday is this week."

A jewelry store! The three musketeers exchanged panicked glances. Abuela said quinceañeras often got jewelry for a present. The Bublassis planned to ruin that, too!

Dom wanted to tell Desmond that he should ask

the dastardly ones to come to the warehouse right now. So they couldn't go to the jeweler. But Desmond stopped her.

"I see you're wearing one of my plungers. I must say, I've never seen them used like that."

"Plungers?" The musketeers were still trying to figure out how the Bublassis knew about the jewels.

"Yes. You're wearing my most expensive model. My company sold the highest number of plungers in the country last year. We found out yesterday. I decided to give a party for my employees, and Vinnie found me three suckling pigs. It seemed as if they came from heaven. Actually, he ordered everything for me, the flowers, the cake. He made everything fall into place."

Desmond turned back toward his car, leaving the musketeers with their jaws almost to their knees. "I hope everything goes well for your party," he said as he got into his car. "I'm sure it will."

"The jewelry!" Dom said when Desmond backed his car away. "It's the jewelry we need to worry about now!" How did Vinnie Bublassi know about the jewelry? He had to have a spy somewhere.

11
The Queen's Diamonds

Dom punched the speaker on the phone. "Rafi!" She could barely get her breath, her heart was pounding so fast. "The queen's diamonds. Vinnie Bublassi has an appointment at a jeweler right now."

"Jeweler?"

Pancho got close to the phone. "Is el Señor Fuentes giving Leni a piece of jewelry that has to be picked up now?"

"Yes . . . yes . . . "

"Rafi!" Dom yelled. "Where are you? This is serious. The Bublassis tried to ruin everything this morning. We know we protected the cake. We think we protected the flowers. But now—now they're heading for the jewelers! What shop? What kind of jewelry is it? Who's going to pick it up?"

"You're right! They could do something. It's her mother's earrings. From when she got married. They're being cleaned and reset at Shiny Baubles. It's the only jeweler in town."

"Who's picking them up, Rafi?"

"I am . . . I was leaving in a few minutes."

"The queen's diamonds," Pancho repeated. "We'll meet you at Yuca, Yuca. Print four copies of the receipt. We'll be there in minutes."

The three musketeers knew about rescuing the queen's diamonds. Steph had seen the movie. Pancho and Dom had read the book—a few times. They took every shortcut they knew and made it to Yuca, Yuca in record time. And Pancho had a plan. He explained it on the way. And it was a good thing they had a plan. Because not far behind them, about a block away, Ernie Bublassi followed.

It was a simple plan. In the book, the boss of the musketeers told them that all four of them should set out to pick up the queen's diamonds in England and bring them back to France. The three musketeers and their friend D'Artagnan set out. Each time bad guys attacked, one musketeer stayed and fought. The others went on. In the end, D'Artagnan was the only one left. He saved the queen's diamonds.

At Yuca, Yuca they told Rafi their plan. Rafi agreed.

Pancho picked up a large bag of long, skinny balloons in his uncle's office, as well as a plastic hand pump. He blew up a few balloons and pocketed the rest, along with the hand pump. He handed Steph a huge bag of wrapped sugar candies from a shelf under the cashier's desk.

Dom, Steph, Pancho, and Rafi started out from Yuca, Yuca. Each with a copy of the Shiny Baubles receipt and directions to the jewelry store. It wasn't all that far, but not that close, either. Like in *The Three Musketeers*, if the Bublassis caught one of them, the others could keep going. In the end, there was a good chance one of the musketeers could get to Shiny Baubles ahead of the meanies.

It worked. The minute they stepped out of Yuca, Yuca, Ernie joined them.

"Whatcha doin' loser-keteers?" the meanie said in a singsong right behind them.

"You didn't know?" Pancho said. "I thought that's why you were here! I'm doing a gig for Yuca, Yuca. Giving away balloon animals to little kids. I do this about once a month." It was the truth.

The musketeers and Rafi surrounded Ernie so he couldn't escape. Dom handed Pancho some of the already inflated balloons. In less than a minute, Pancho and Dom twisted red balloons around Ernie's ankles to hold them together, orange ones around his knees, and yellow ones in between. Steph wrapped elaborate handcuffs around his hands and wrists. Then she made them even more secure when she tied an uninflated balloon around his wrists. Tight.

The balloons were surprisingly strong. Now Ernie couldn't move without bursting them. Which would make a lot of noise. The musketeers bet Ernie wouldn't want that kind of attention.

As the musketeers worked, Rafi blew up a few more balloons. Pancho wove them and mixed them to make a fantastical multicolored helmet. Rafi plopped it on Ernie's head, almost covering his eyes. For a finishing touch, Pancho twisted two balloons together to make a guard to cover Ernie's mouth.

"Thanks for helping me," he said. "You can just stand here." Then he called out to everyone on the street. "Step right up! Free balloon animals! A gift from Yuca, Yuca, the best Cuban restaurant in Mundytown. Step right up!"

"SWehogpktft!" Ernie said. But he couldn't move his feet without bursting the balloons, and the balloons in his hands and wrists didn't let him take off the guard over his mouth.

Pancho tucked a dog balloon under Ernie's arm. "Here—hold this puppy dog. Everybody loves this one."

Little kids began to line up, and Pancho got going with his show.

After Dom took a picture of the balloon man, she, Steph, and Rafi continued on to Shiny Baubles.

❧ ❧ ❧

Ponsi joined them two blocks after they left Pancho and Ernie. Had the Bublassis stationed themselves along the route to the jewelers?

The two musketeers, Rafi, and Ponsi walked in silence for about half a block. Which was when Steph decided to pull the jumbo bag of candy from her shoulder bag.

"Forsooth!" she told Ponsi. "Look at all this candy. Mayhap we should give it to these worthy citizens. Please, kind sir, help me."

"Me?" Ponsi pointed to his chest.

"You owe me!" Steph whispered. "Remember my leg brace? Now is your chance to do right. You don't help me, I'll let everyone know how you took it away and Dom and Pancho had to rescue me when we were on our knightly adventure."

"Right!" Ponsi said, trying to get away. "Who's everyone?"

"Kind lady." Dom ignored Ponsi's question and stepped toward a woman on the street. "The musketeer is trying to distribute these gifts to all the passersby, but this young knave won't help her."

"He is most dastardly," Rafi added.

People stopped out of curiosity.

Ponsi tried to get around them.

Dom quickly pulled her phone out of her pocket. "You may not care about these other people, but I bet you'll care if Mr. Franklin Desmond gets wind of it. And I bet that kind gentleman would be only too happy to tell your mother," she said. "They talk to each other often, right? They live in the same abode?"

Ponsi stopped. He sighed. "Okay, okay, okay. I'll help you already. But it won't be for long."

"Tell Mr. Desmond and your mother 'Hi' for us." Dom and Rafi left Steph and Ponsi handing out candy and continued on their way to Shiny Baubles.

❧ ❧ ❧

Dom and Rafi walked and talked like brother and sister, which of course, they were.

"If it isn't the two Melendez losers." It was Vinnie Bublassi.

"Vinnie," Dom said. "How nice to see you."

"Hey, Vinnie," Rafi said. "What's up?"

"I heard you'd be going to the jewelry store. I

figured I'd join you and keep you company on your way," the dastardly Bublassi said.

"Jewelry store?" Rafi said. "Are you going to a jewelry store, Musketeer? I'm delivering this envelope to one of Mom's clients. I promised her I'd do it before I went home to get dressed for the party."

"Yeah, right!"

"I'm not going to a jewelry store either," Dom said. "I'm heading to a craft store to buy beads to decorate my hat. I want it even more special for the party tonight," she said, even though she wasn't invited.

"You guys really think I believe you?"

Dom and Rafi both shrugged. At the end of the block, they turned in opposite directions. "See you at home, Dom," Rafi said.

Dom doffed her hat in salute.

Vinnie Bublassi hesitated. It was easy to see he didn't know who to follow. Neither of them was going in the direction of the jewelry store.

After a few seconds, he followed Rafi.

It would have worked either way. If Vinnie had followed Dom, she would go to the craft store and waste some time—Rafi, then, would go to the jeweler. Since Vinnie followed Rafi, Dom hurried to the jewelry store. She came out about half an hour later, carrying a small glittery bag with a velvet box nestled in silver tissue paper.

The three Bublassi brothers waited for her on the sidewalk. All winded. As if each had run a long race.

"I'll take that bag now," Vinnie told Dom. "Tell Leni she can come get this at my house after her party."

Dom's hands trembled. She tried to move her hands, which held the bag, away from the meanies. But the Bublassis were everywhere. Her eyes filled. There was nothing she could do. "Leni doesn't know anything about this. It's a surprise from her grandfather. They belonged to her mother. Can't you have pity on the poor girl?"

"Pity? No time for pity. Her grandfather didn't have pity for me when he told my mother why he fired me." Vinnie swiped the bag out of Dom's hands. "We need to go now," he said. "We have an appointment at twelve thirty."

"You know—" Dom sniffed. "You know—this is stealing. I'm going to call the police about this."

"You won't," Vinnie said. "Especially if Leni doesn't know. You don't want to upset her, do you? And I told you, I'm just borrowing it. She can have it back after the party." Then he snarled, "And this isn't the last you'll see of us."

Ponsi and Ernie stuck their tongues out at her, as if they were still in kindergarten. "See you at the community center, loser-keteer!"

12
The Community Fortress

Dom finally made it to the community center, minutes after Steph and Roco. Steph had stopped at home to get their steed. All three of them hurried over to the party room. Earlier, Leni and her friends had dressed each table with cascades of blue and purple flowers. They had set out the finest china the community center owned. Streamers decorated windows and doors. All the drapes were tied back with deep-purple velvet cords.

"So?" Steph asked Dom the minute Dom stepped into the room.

"It worked perfectly. The jeweler said Pancho picked up the real earrings and left ten minutes before I got there. Vinnie Bublassi followed Rafi, but all three Bublassis met me when I came out and demanded I give them my bag. I cried a bit. And threatened to call the police." Dom put her hand to her forehead in mock despair. "They stuck their tongues out at me. But they are now the proud owners of a gorgeous pair of fake earrings the jewelers use in their shop window."

Steph snickered. "Good job! Now we just wait for Pancho."

"No, no, no, no!" Dom said. "We can't just wait for Pancho."

"But he rode his bike. All he had to do was drop off the earrings at Yuca, Yuca. He should be here any minute."

"No, no. That's not what I mean. We can't just wait for Pancho! Vinnie said they'd see us at the community center. They haven't finished messing with the party!"

"The fortress?" Steph asked.

"The fortress!"

The fortress was like the queen's diamonds. Another way the real musketeers had fooled their enemies.

"We need to dress some sticks into dummies."

"Right. Brooms or mops or something. And attach them to chairs."

They prowled the halls. They found a mop in the janitor's closet. The janitor said they could use it.

They found a broom under the piano. They figured they could use it because no one else was.

They hustled upstairs. They met Mrs. Kiddo, the person in charge of the children's room. Dom knew her from summer camp. They told Mrs. Kiddo their problem. "Could we borrow costumes for the afternoon? We'll put them back exactly where we found them," Dom said.

"Take your choice." Mrs. Kiddo opened a closet filled with clothes and costumes. She pointed them to drawers full of paper clips, spools of string, and all sorts of tape. She let them use a long stick she kept for limbo contests.

Dom's eyes lit up. "Ooh, ooh!" She pointed to a bunch of hats on the top shelf. "If we use your hats, we'll still be able to wear ours!"

Steph frowned. "They don't have feathers. . . ."

"Oh yeah . . ."

Mrs. Kiddo pointed to Steph's hat. "Why don't you take that big plume and attach it to just one of the hats?"

"The lights are not on in the ballroom. . . . They might be fooled by just one hat. . . ."

"They won't pay that much attention. . . ."

"Perfect!" Dom decided.

"Perfect!" Steph agreed.

They settled down to make the dummies. They stuffed plastic grocery bags with paper from the recycling bin to make the heads, and taped the bags to the top of the sticks. They taped coat hangers wearing jackets under the "heads" and tied scarves around the neck where they joined. Steph took the stubby plume and transferred it to one of

Mrs. Kiddo's hats. In very little time three dummy musketeers were ready. Mrs. Kiddo helped the girls take them down to the ballroom.

Steph and Dom thanked Mrs. Kiddo. They settled the dummies on one of the tables. They fussed and tried different poses to make sure they fooled anyone who tried to spy through the windows. Dom used a pin to attach the coat sleeve of one dummy to the tablecloth so it would look more natural.

"And where do you think Pancho is?" Steph asked Dom once they were done.

Pancho should have been there by now, Dom knew. But she didn't want to believe the Bublassis had done something to him. "He'll be here soon. Don't worry. Maybe he decided to go home first."

"You don't think the Bublassis stopped him, do you? And took Leni's earrings?"

"I'm sure they didn't," Dom said, although she wasn't sure at all. She was scared to death for Pancho, but if she said it aloud, it might seem more real than it already was. "Let's go outside and check out our defenses."

* * *

They weren't surprised at what they saw when they opened the door. Pancho racing toward the community center. His teal plume was totally gone, and a white bag dangled from his bike's handlebars.

"They're after me! They're after me!" he yelled as he dropped his bike at the steps.

"Is that the earrings?" Dom pointed to the bag.

Pancho struggled to catch his breath. "Long story. The Bublassis must not have gone to Desmond's warehouse. They were waiting for me when I came out of Yuca, Yuca. I pedaled as fast as I could, but I'm sure they're only a couple of blocks away!"

"The fortress!" Dom and Steph yelled.

"The fortress?" Pancho said. "Awesome! Except they can already see we're here."

Pancho was right. Dom could see two boys running toward the community center. She couldn't see their faces yet, but she could see their shirts— the same color as the ones they'd worn earlier. It had to be Ernie and Ponsi. And if she could see the bullies, the bullies could see them. The dummies wouldn't work. And the musketeers weren't ready anyway. "We'll just talk our way out of it."

Dom walked down the steps.

"Forsooth, do you come to parlay?" she yelled as the Bublassis came through the community center gate.

"Do you wanna talk?" Pancho translated from the top of the steps.

"Move it, featherhead. We have business inside. And we need to do it fast. We have another party to go to." The two bullies stopped in the middle of the community center's yard.

"I'll give you a chance to go back to Desmond's party, and we promise to be mum about this day," Dom said. "Let the maiden have her feast. Go on your way!"

"We don't care if the maiden has her feast!" Ponsi Bublassi yelled. "Move it or . . ."

"Mayhap you'd sing a different tune if you knew the janitor and Mrs. Kiddo know of your dastardly deeds. They're prepared to stop you," Steph said.

"Like we're afraid of them."

Dom pulled out her phone. "Then mayhap I should call Frank Desmond and tell him you skipped out on helping him set up for his party!"

"Wh—aaaah?"

Dom brought her phone to her face. "Cheeese!"

She clicked and then waved her phone in her stretched-out arm. "Maybe earlier you didn't believe Franklin Desmond, a gentleman of your acquaintance, is in my contact list."

"I'm sure your mother would be interested to know how helpful you *weren't* today," Pancho warned.

"And about all your plans to ruin the maiden's party," Steph added.

Ernie shifted from one leg to the other. "Uh, uh . . ."

Ponsi waved his brother's fears away. "She won't."

Dom's eyebrows rose. In plain sight of the boys, she selected the picture. Slowly, carefully, she turned the phone and punched a couple of times. Then she let her index finger hover dramatically over the screen. "Watch me!"

"Stop! No!" Ernie yelled. He turned toward his

brother. "She knows too much. She's gonna do it."

Ponsi shook his head. "You got away with it this time, featherhead. But we're coming back. And our brother Vinnie's coming back with us. You'll be sorry!"

"Make sure you tell Mr. Desmond a good story!" Pancho said. "I'm sure he wants to know why you're not helping him get ready for his party."

As the two bullies walked away, the musketeers could hear Ernie. "She really does know a lot."

Dom plopped down on the bottom step. "Dastardly disaster dodged!"

"Indeed!" Steph agreed. "But not for long."

Pancho told about what happened after Dom and Steph left him covering Ernie in balloons. He'd kept Ernie for at least fifteen minutes, until the dastardly Bublassi finally worked himself out of his "chains." Ernie followed the same direction that Dom and Steph and Rafi had taken. Quickly Pancho hopped on his bike. He made it to the jeweler in a flash and then returned to the restaurant to hand the precious cargo to the waiting Señor Fuentes. That's when he found malanga fritters on the menu and decided to wait till they were ready, to bring some to the musketeers for lunch.

"You mean you worried us to death for some kind of greasy fritters?" Steph's voice sounded annoyed.

"Not just any kind of fritters. Malanga fritters!" Pancho pulled the white bag off his bike's handlebars and handed out the treats.

"And what are ma-lahn-gah fritters made from?" Steph still hadn't tasted hers.

Dom and Pancho looked at each other.

"No clue," Pancho said.

"Beats me," Dom said.

"And you guys eat things that you have no idea what they are?"

"If they taste good."

"And you've been eating them your whole life."

"It's not like it's intestines or anything," Dom said as she munched. "It's a vegetable. I know that much."

Steph took a tentative bite. "Mmmm. Malanga fritters," she said. "Worth the worry."

While they chomped, Steph told them about patting her pockets pretending to look for her phone every time Ponsi threatened to leave her. She kept him handing out candy until Ernie rescued him. They followed the direction Rafi and Dom had taken.

When the malanga fritters were gone, the musketeers cleaned up their mess, rearranged the hats on their dummies, and planned what to do once the Bublassis came back.

But they didn't know when that would be.

So they stationed themselves at windows.

Upstairs.

So they could see anyone who approached the community center.

Pancho spotted the dastardly ones at about three thirty. They were dressed up. Ready for the plunger party.

"Places," he yelled on his way downstairs. "Lucky us, they're coming through the back."

Steph and Dom ran outside through the front door.

Steph dove under a huge clump of rhododendrons with her weapon. She was close to the right side of the building with a perfect view of the community center's backyard.

Dom sneaked into the canopy of the magnolia tree on the left of the building. From that spot, between the branches, she could see the back too. *And* she was next to an open window so that when she gave the signal, Pancho would hear it.

Pancho slid down the railing of the basement steps like he'd been doing since he was six. He went to summer camp there too. He stationed himself where he could hear Dom's signal.

The three Bublassis stopped close to the back door.

"Featherhead's gone," Vinnie said loud enough for Dom to hear. "She would have been out here by now if she was in the building."

"I bet they thought we weren't coming back," Ponsi added.

Ernie took a few careful steps toward the building and looked through a window. He turned around quickly to meet his brothers. "They're in the party room. Sitting around a table. It's dark, but I can see them through the window—they're still wearing the crazy musketeer hats!"

"Now we'll show them what it's like to mess with the Bublassis!" Ponsi said.

"You guys know what to do," Vinnie reminded his brothers. "There's a hose on either side. I'll go open the windows for you."

All three Bublassis took off.

But the musketeers beat them at their own game.

"One for all!" Dom yelled.

From under the rhododendrons, Steph pulled the trigger on her hose. Her aim was perfect. Spray blasted Ernie's face and soaked his checkered party shirt. The torrent swept over every inch of him, especially his shoes. They wanted the Bublassis to squish all the way home to slow them down. When she was sure Ernie was soaked, Steph aimed at Vinnie.

At the exact same time as Steph, Dom pulled the trigger on her hose from the branches of the magnolia. The water surged toward Ponsi, drowning his hair and his face and pouring over his shirt and pants. She also flooded his shoes. She aimed at Vinnie as soon as she was satisfied Ponsi was drenched.

The boys ran. They tried to get away from the sprays. That's when Pancho executed their brilliant move.

He turned on the sprinklers. Full blast!

If there was a dry place on any of the three Bublassis, it disappeared.

"All for one!" came Dom's signal after a minute.

The hoses and the sprinklers stopped.

Pancho and Roco ran out to the community center's wet backyard. Steph crawled out from under the rhododendrons, and Dom hopped down from the tree.

"Would you like me to call the honorable Monsieur Desmond to pick you up?" she asked. "Mayhap you'll need to change robes before his party."

13
Three Musketeers with Panache

The musketeers put back the hoses and swept the back steps and walkway so no one would slip. They helped unload the truck when el Señor Prieto arrived with the roasted pigs and other food from Yuca, Yuca. They organized the place cards and fixed the deep-purple bows on the backs of the chairs.

"I wish we could stay," Steph said.

"I wouldn't mind seeing what it's like," Dom agreed.

"We could offer to patrol the grounds," Pancho suggested.

They got their wish.

El Señor Fuentes rushed into the hall.

"A terrible misunderstanding," he said. "The people who were supposed to come to serve the appetizers were booked at a party to celebrate toilet plungers!"

"TOILET PLUNGERS?" the musketeers echoed in a chorus.

"Yes, yes, yes!" The eyebrows over el Señor Fuentes's blue eye and brown eye both danced wildly. "A terrible misunderstanding. Who would have a party to celebrate toilet plungers?"

"Somebody who wanted to take away your helpers!" Pancho added. The Bublassis finally got away with something.

"Exactly, mi amigo." The eyebrows still jumped around. "They were supposed to be here half an hour ago. Your uncle just called them, and that's what they told him. Toilet plungers!"

"We could help," Dom said. "We'll tidy up our musketeer outfits and pass around the appetizers."

"We'll be happy to help in the kitchen now," Steph added.

"All you need to do is show us," Pancho finished.

And they did.

Once the appetizers were all prepared, el Señor Fuentes took them by his store to make dressier baldrics. He let them choose more jewels to adorn their hats. They each ran home for a quick change.

Dom called Abuela as she put on party duds and told her all that had happened.

"Ay, mi amor, how exciting. Emilio Fuentes will be so grateful for what you did!"

Dom told her about how el Señor Fuentes didn't really know all they'd done and how they were now about to serve the appetizers.

"You must pass the appetizers with *panache*," Abuela said.

"Panache?" Dom asked.

"Like they are the most important and glamorous thing in the world, my dear. Like you're a movie star!"

"Panache!" Dom said with conviction. "Got it!"

They stood by the community center's kitchen when Leni made her grand entrance, in violet satin and sequins, along with her court. On Rafi's arm, she glowed. Her mother's earrings sparkled beneath her shiny brown hair. Rafi's smile was so big, Dom was sure she could see his tonsils. El Señor Fuentes's eyes were full.

And during the party, the musketeers passed the appetizers with panache. When they weren't passing around appetizers, they guarded the entrances. Everyone commented on how helpful and efficient they were. When the dancing started, the musketeers joined the party on the dance floor.

Leni stopped them and told them it was the best day of her life.

"You just don't know how much it meant to me that you helped with the appetizers. It could have been so much worse!"

Dom glanced at the others. If Leni only knew!

Leni, Rafi, el Señor Fuentes, and the musketeers sat on the front steps of the community center after everyone had left.

"I understand you did a lot more than help with the appetizers," el Señor Fuentes finally said.

"A little," Dom said modestly. "It wasn't much, really."

"It wasn't much?" Rafi exclaimed. "You just figured out that the dastardly Bublassis wanted to mess up the whole party . . . and you stopped them from doing it!"

"Show them," Steph said. "Show them our pictures."

And Dom did. "What I don't understand is how they knew about the earrings. And the servers for the appetizers."

"I can fill that in," Rafi said.

Everyone's eyes focused on Rafi.

"When Vinnie finally figured out I was actually delivering spreadsheets for Mami, he got furious," Rafi said. "He started yelling at the top of his lungs even though he didn't have to. I was right there next to him."

Vinnie told Rafi he'd always planned on a random dastardly deed to get back at el Señor Fuentes for getting him in trouble with his mom. He found out that Tava's Butcher had Leni's pigs on the same day he found out about Desmond's plunger party, which also happened to be the day Dom showed up with the check. "The easiest thing was to talk Desmond into buying the pigs."

Rafi stopped for a minute and looked at Leni, making a pitiful face. "It was Emily," he said. "And you were right, Sis. He'd already been working on it, but when you came in with the check, he had the perfect way to do it and not get in trouble." Then Rafi looked at Leni. "Vinnie knew that you and Emily were friends, and he knew that Emily loved to talk. He sweet-talked her, and Emily was really impressed a football player *and* a senior was talking to her. She gave him all the details without even knowing what she was doing."

Rafi explained how the musketeers kept messing up Vinnie's plans. Every time the musketeers stopped them, the Bublassis needed to do more.

Vinnie took off running after he got the whole story off his chest. And in the end, the Bublassis ended up all wet.

"I have plenty of material and pictures for a great book for Abuela," Rafi said when he finished.

"And what will your next adventure be, Musketeers?" el Señor Fuentes asked. His eyebrows were very, very relaxed.

"I don't know," Dom said. "I'm kind of itching for a mystery!"

Pancho and Steph raised their plungers in agreement.

"I have a perfect magnifying glass for you," the salvage man said.

Author's Note

All for One is inspired by *The Three Musketeers*, a book written in 1844 by French author Alexandre Dumas. In turn, *The Three Musketeers* is very loosely based on a real person, Charles de Batz-Castelmore, and three other high-ranking nobles who served in the court of Louis XIII in the 1600s.

Dumas was the grandson of a marquis, a French nobleman who married a slave from Haiti. His father fought for Napoleon. Alexandre, himself, was a scribe—a writer—for the Duke of Orleans, who later became King Louis Philippe of France. He worked for the duke during a revolution in France in 1830.

The Three Musketeers was published in a Paris newspaper one chapter at a time from March through July of 1844. Each chapter was a complete scene, woven into a whole story, each with a cliffhanger at the end to keep the readers buying the newspaper.

The story took place while King Louis XIII was king of France. D'Artagnan, a young man from the country, came to Paris to become a musketeer. On his first day in Paris, he ran into three men who were already musketeers. Three friends. Unfortunately, he made the musketeers unhappy. Each for a different reason. The three challenged D'Artagnan to duels, one after the other. But dueling was against the law. And they were caught. D'Artagnan sided with the musketeers. He was such a good swordsman, he helped them beat the law, and they all escaped.

The four became friends forever, and D'Artagnan became a musketeer at the end of the book.

The musketeers' headquarters was at L'Hotel de Ville, and their slogan was "One for all and all for one." I chose *All for One* as the name of this book because everyone, just everyone, was working to make Leni's party a success.

Like Dom, Pancho, and Steph, the real musketeers valued honor and tried to help those in need. They often got out of jams by fast-talking and confusing people using just a bit of truth spoken with conviction—like Steph, Dom, and Pancho did at Tava's Butcher. The musketeers were also very interested in love. There were many people who loved one another and people who were scorned by lovers in the book, but also, there was revenge.

The musketeers pledged themselves to defend the queen, like Dom, Steph, and Pancho pledged themselves to help Leni.

Two scenes in *All for One* are based on famous scenes in *The Three Musketeers*. In the first, the musketeers and D'Artagnan set out to bring the queen's diamonds, which were in England, back to France. The four of them rode out together. As their enemies attacked them along the way, one musketeer stayed and fought while the others went on. Only D'Artagnan reached England, retrieved the queen's diamonds, and returned them to the queen in Paris. Like in our book, there were real diamonds and fake diamonds, and the musketeers foiled their enemies.

The second instance took place during a war with England. The English invaded a French island—

the Isle of Rhé—near the town of La Rochelle. The French citizens of La Rochelle sided with England, which caused King Louis XIII and his armies to attack. One of the battles was at a place called the Bastion Saint-Gervais. The bastion—a fortress—was destroyed, but the Rochellais still guarded it. The three musketeers and D'Artagnan, looking for a place to talk undisturbed about important matters, made a bet that they could spend an hour in the destroyed bastion without getting killed. Soldiers from La Rochelle attacked twice. And twice the four drove them back. When, finally, a whole regiment attacked, the musketeers and D'Artagnan had their helper pose dead soldiers with muskets so the attackers could see them. They then escaped through the back while the "battle" raged.

When Dom and her crew ask Desmond to imprison the Bublassis in a tower far away, they echo the latter part of the musketeers' story. The most despicable villain in the book, a woman who plotted and ruined many lives, was imprisoned in England by her brother-in-law. She was kept in a faraway castle, in a room high over the sea, until a young man she enthralled saved her. She was caught again and ended up dead. At least the Bublassis only ended up wet.

Turn the page for a sneak peek
at Dominguita's next adventure!

What the Note Said

Dominguita Melendez was up and out the door early on Thursday morning. She was on her way to Yuca, Yuca, the best Cuban restaurant in Mundytown. It was also the only Cuban restaurant in Mundytown. Dom had a deal with the owner, el Señor Prieto: Dom swept the store's sidewalk; el Señor Prieto provided lunch for her crew during their adventures.

Today she hoped el Señor Prieto would give her

a lunch-to-go even though the crew wasn't going on an adventure. Just Dom and Steph were going on a weekend trip to Steph's grandmother's house—on the Rappa River.

"It might be the last good food I get till we get back," she told el Señor Prieto.

"You think? Pancho tells me that Steph's grandmother makes great chocolate chip cookies." Pancho was the third member of Dom's crew. He was also el Señor Prieto's nephew.

"Steph called it a cabin . . . out in the country . . . on a river. . . . She said it's next to a marsh." Dom raised her eyebrows. "What if it doesn't even have a kitchen? And you know what? There are no Pizza Palaces out in the country."

"No!"

Dom nodded with force to make sure el Señor Prieto got her point. "By a river? Near a marsh? Nah. No Pizza Palaces."

El Señor Prieto shrugged. He picked out a plate of figure-eight pastries shining with syrup—buñuelos—Dom's and Pancho's favorite food. As if by magic,

Pancho stepped out of the restaurant's kitchen.

"I wish I could go with you." Pancho reached for one of his uncle's delicious pastries along with a napkin. He was invited, like Dom, to Gran's river house for the long weekend, but his family was going to see his own grandmother.

Dom wanted to make Pancho feel better. She stopped chomping on her buñuelo. "It's not like we'll have any adventures," she said, wiping sticky syrup from her chin. "I couldn't even find the place on the map. *Tapperville!* I'm sure *nothing* will happen there. And we'll be back in no time."

"Just in case." Pancho handed her a piece of paper with his mother's number. "Call me if something happens. I want to be in on the planning. And figuring things out. I want to be part of it all even if I'm not there."

"I'll call you if we get into trouble," she told Pancho. "But really, we won't have any adventures. This place is a million miles from anywhere. Steph and I are taking Sherlock Holmes books. That's about the only excitement we'll have."

Pancho headed home—his shoulders slumped, his head down.

Dom didn't know what to do for him, he looked so sad.

She also didn't know what she would do without him. Before their knightly adventure, Dom hadn't needed friends. She'd found plenty of friends and adventures in her books. But then Pancho had become her squire and Steph, her master of the cookies. She loved her new friends and the adventures she had with them.

Really loved them.

But there was no time to feel sad. She had to get to work. She grabbed the broom and swept the sidewalk. Once she was done, she picked up the bag of food and thanked el Señor Prieto. The smell of ham croquettes and malanga fritters followed her home.

ٯ ٯ ٯ

As Dom walked home, she got a call from Abuela. Which was unusual. First because it was early. And second because Abuela now forgot a lot of things.

Dom was normally the one to make the calls. But Abuela sounded sharp today. "It's very important that you behave well," she said. "The family's honor is on your shoulders. And if you don't behave well, that girl, that girl . . ."

"Steph."

"Yeah. Steph. And her grandmother. They'll think Cuban kids don't know how to behave. You're representing Cuban kids everywhere, you know."

The family's honor? Cubans kids everywhere? It was true that Dom had never been away from her family. But really? She was only spending a long weekend! Dom bet her mami had put Abuela up to it.

She was already worried about the food, and now she had to worry about the family's honor and the honor of every Cuban kid in the universe! She had been excited to go, but it was getting complicated. She was happy that her brother, Rafi, knew exactly what to say when she got home.

"Don't forget," he said. "If you find adventures, take pictures. And take notes. So I can write a book for Abuela . . . *if* you find an adventure."

Steph and her grandmother, Gran, picked Dom up at exactly eight thirty. Which meant Dom's head was still full of warnings when she got in the car. Even though Dom suspected a Mami-Abuela conspiracy, her mami had added to what Abuela said. The warnings ricocheted so fast she felt her head would explode. And Steph didn't help. She fell asleep two blocks after Dom got in the car.

"Don't you want to take a little snooze?" Gran asked. Dom could see her smile in the rearview mirror. It was clear Gran didn't want to chitchat. Dom took out her phone and added Pancho's number into her contacts.

Mami had given her the phone when Abuela had to move to Miami to live with her sister, because Abuela was forgetting lots and lots of things. Without Abuela, Dom would be home alone after school. At first Dom was supposed to use the phone only to let Mami know she was safe or if she was abducted by aliens. But Dom missed Abuela. She used the phone to stay in touch. And to solve problems in their adventures. And to take pictures that her brother, Rafi, used to illustrate books he wrote for Abuela. The books were about Dom's adventures—to help Abuela feel like she was still close to Dom and Rafi.

Dom put her phone away. And tried to look out the window. But worry began to snake into her brain. She was good at that. Worrying.

She worried about the cabin. She loved wildlife— during the day. But if a daddy longlegs strolled across her forehead and took a jump on her lips while she was asleep, she might just go through the roof. If a mouse ran across her belly, she would have to burst through the door. That would not be good for the family's honor.

And what if the cabin had no indoor bathrooms? She wasn't looking forward to battling bats and sidestepping snakes to take care of business. She might have to hold it all night to protect the honor of all the Cuban kids who ever existed.

She wished she'd asked Steph a lot more questions before she'd decided to come. But with Steph asleep,

Dom would have to wait until she got to Gran's cabin to know what was what.

The best thing she could do was read.

Dom dove into her favorite Sherlock Holmes story. She didn't come up for air until she felt the car slow down into back roads. They drove through pastures broken by groves of trees. Farm houses, barns, even a few creaky windmills. Cows and sheep and goats. Not at all like the building-crammed streets of Mundytown, where she lived.

After the welcome sign for Tapperville, Gran really slowed down. Dom was happily surprised to see a Pizza Palace as they drove down the main road! Soon Gran turned. Her tires crunched on a long gravel driveway to a beautiful white house. It was a little like Gran's house in Mundytown. Plants dressed in leaves of different greens, yellows, and purples wrapped around a porch that wrapped around the house—a colorful outdoor room full of bright yellow rocking chairs. The steps leading to the porch were dark green and shiny.

Is this the house? she mouthed to Steph, who woke when the car slowed down.

Steph nodded.

PHEW!!!!

Gran helped the girls unload the bags and coolers onto the driveway and handed Steph the key.

"I'll be right back," she said.

"We know what to do," Steph said. Then she turned to Dom. "She's going to town to pick up the mail. We can take a minute to look around the yard, but if we take things in, it makes her really happy."

They walked between peach trees and apple trees. Steph showed her Gran's pie patch—raspberry and blueberry bushes bordered with new rhubarb plants.

"Gran and my grandfather used to live here while my grandfather was alive. When he died, my parents talked Gran into moving to Mundytown. But she still spends a lot of time here in the summer."

As Steph showed her around, Dom noted everything in her head. Including a not-so-big gray building that Steph called the barn. Behind it, the marsh seemed to go on forever. And she especially noticed what wasn't there—an outhouse.

"We spend a lot of time in the garden when we're here," Steph explained as they stepped onto the porch. "Did you bring Sherlock Holmes like you said you would?"

Dom nodded. "I read all the way here."

"Gran has a copy. We can come out here and read till she gets back."

"No time for reading," Dom said.

She had seen a note tacked to the door:

ESTHER STOLEN

NEED HELP